# BURN
Holly S. Roberts

FourCaratPress.com

*Holly S. Roberts*

**BURN**
Holly S. Roberts

Published by Four Carat Press
Copyright 2016 Holly S. Roberts

Printing History
eBook edition 2016
Paperback edition 2016

Edited by Michelle Kowalski
Cover by Fantasia Frog Designs

This is a work of fiction. ALL characters are derived from the author's imagination.

No person, brand, or corporation mentioned in this Book should be taken to have endorsed this Book nor should the events surrounding them be considered in any way factual.

## Dedication

To Loyd and Sue

Thank you for your dedication to booklovers in Arizona.
You kept my dream alive and I'm honored to know you.

Please visit this incredible bookstore and tell them Holly sent you.

BookKrazy
1609 E. Bell Rd. B6
Phoenix, AZ 85022
602-867-1018
www.bookkrazy.com

# PROLOGUE

*Dax*

**She is so beautiful**. The inner glow she carries can light up a room. Her rounded tummy is swollen with our child—a boy, according to the ultrasound. We chose the name Mason Dax Montgomery. If, on the slim chance the ultrasound is wrong, her name will be Masey Savannah Montgomery.

I took half the day off work to drive my wife, Savannah, to the seven-month obstetrician appointment. We are both excited and basking in the bright rays of pending parenthood. I never dreamed about anything as incredible as Savannah having my baby.

We eat cereal for breakfast—Savannah has one bowl covered in bananas and I enjoy two, minus the bananas. Her pregnancy brings about cravings for the yellow fruit, and it has become one of my favorite ways to tease her.

"I have a really big banana for you," I tell her with the best leer I can manage. She blushes and we both laugh at the joke I've said over and over since three or four bananas a day became her go-to pregnancy food. She loves me even when I'm a goof and that love makes my world go round.

I was the rough, blue-collar worker from a dysfunctional family. My mom, Dad's daily punching bag, died of cancer when I was ten, and my father drank himself to death when I was seventeen. Savannah was the spoiled rich girl who gave up everything for me. She might blush but she loves my sexually explicit teasing. We love each other, and hearing the baby's heartbeat and counting down the last weeks until we hold our precious bundle is all we care about.

I rinse and put the dishes in the dishwasher while she adds makeup to a face that needs none. After cleaning the tabletop, I head back to our room in the small two bedroom house we rented. One room for us and a room for the baby is all we need. We bought a crib the week before. Savannah put in hours online making sure the crib was safe, while I put in overtime so we could buy the one she wanted. I painted the walls a soft purple because Savannah loves the color. She has lists of all the things we still need. I will continue working overtime and buy each one. It means everything to me that I can provide for her and our baby.

I enter the bedroom and Savannah is standing in front of the bathroom mirror. I walk through the door, wrap my arms around her, rest my hands on her tummy, and then kiss behind her ear at the hairline. This kiss is usually a score. She melts back against my chest, the makeup wand thing-y lifted.

"We don't have time and I think you have a serious kink for fat women," she says in her husky sex voice.

"Only my fat woman," I whisper back and kiss the exact spot again.

"You're cruel." She smiles into the mirror.

I rest my chin on her head. "I refuse to argue over your size anymore. Soon you'll be the size of a house and I'll still want you."

She places the wand thing-y down and turns in my arms, laughing. She kisses my chin. "You are evil. I will not be as big as a house."

I look down at her extended belly wondering how it can actually grow larger. Savannah was such a tiny little thing. She didn't even show her pregnancy until a month ago. Then, she exploded. Even her cheeks got pudgy, and like I said before, she's beautiful. I might not be the most intelligent man but I keep thoughts of pudgy cheeks and exploding bellies to myself.

"Smart man not to say what you're thinking," she laughs and gives me a small push.

"Who me?" I pull her close again and kiss the sweetest lips on the planet. Her lips. Our child. My Savannah.

Our playful and loving mood continues into the doctor's office. We listen to the baby's heartbeat, and Savannah asks questions about what to expect during her last two months of pregnancy. Not that she really needs answers. She has read every book available on the subject. I know this because she reviews everything she discovers with me each night when I arrive home from work. I listen and make appropriate comments. I do my best to look interested and not exhausted from all the overtime I'm putting in. She knows this and she appreciates my attention. I always see it in her eyes—her love for me and our baby. The doctor answers all Savannah's questions with a patient smile. You can't help smiling back at my Savannah. Her love for life is infectious.

After we leave the office, she's bubbly with excitement and also hungry. I don't really have time to take her to lunch. The disappointment on her face changes my mind. My boss won't fire me, but it's obvious he doesn't understand my need to attend her doctor appointments. He's old school, while I'm infatuated with pending fatherhood and can't wait to attend our baby's birth.

With my family history, all I care about is giving my child a father to be proud of. I want everything for him, everything I never had. Come hell or high water, he will have a home with two loving parents and a chance at being more than a blue-collar laborer.

After we leave the restaurant, Savannah chats on about the upcoming birthing classes. For her, it's another step closer to our child's arrival. For me, it's waking up an hour earlier in the morning so I can leave work an hour earlier at night and attend the classes. Seeing her so happy helps alleviate the constant stress I'm under.

My light is green and I'm doing about thirty miles per hour when I pass through the intersection. The car comes out of nowhere. The first thing that registers is the impact—the grinding and crunching of metal and my body straining against the seat belt as I'm thrown forward and back. Almost simultaneously, the car fills with Savannah's scream. We are both wearing seat belts, but our old car doesn't have airbags. Then, everything goes quiet except Savannah gasping for breath. She's bent forward holding her belly. I unclick her seat belt and place my hand on her arm. Her panic-filled eyes stare back at me.

"It's okay," I say while shutting off the engine. The car immediately starts heating up because it's summer in Phoenix and over a hundred degrees outside. I don't want the engine sparking a gas fire. We're okay, just shaken up, I tell myself.

Savannah isn't talking. Her eyes are so large and her lips move like she's trying to form words. It dawns on me that something is terribly wrong.

"Is it the baby?" I ask her.

She looks at me and continues with the same strange gasping noises. I unbuckle my seat belt and throw open the door. The back passenger door took the main impact, so I run around the front of the car and open Savannah's door. Her head is turned away from me. I know I shouldn't move her, but all I can think of is wrapping her in my arms. Her face is now tinged blue and her eyes vacant. My shocked brain realizes the cement is too hot to lay her down. I place her back in the seat and grab the seat adjuster to push it back as far as it will go. I frantically do chest compressions and breathe air into her lungs. I hear a wounded animal sound and finally realize it's coming from me.

Savannah doesn't respond, her beautiful eyes stare at nothing. No, this can't be happening. I look around and squint into the sun. I notice the driver's door of the car that hit us opening. I'm desperate and refuse to believe she's gone. We need help. Someone must save my Savannah. I run around his car and approach the other driver hoping he has a cell phone. Having a cell phone is not in our budget at the moment, and I'm kicking myself for not working more overtime to get one. Two things stand out: sirens in the distance and the man at his vehicle.

"I didn't mean to hit you," he slurs.

"Do you have…" I start to ask about his cell phone, when he belches and the strong odor of alcohol reaches me.

Blackness fills me and rage takes over.

I don't remember pulling my knife or stabbing the driver thirteen times. The next thing I know, pain like I've never felt makes my entire body seize, and I fall to the ground. My world is a dark blur and it's only later that I learn a cop's Taser took me down. He should have shot me through the heart and ended the pain.

Savannah and our son died because the other driver decided to drive drunk. The impact caused the sac holding the baby to rupture and amniotic fluid to fill Savannah's lungs. My wife drowned. And, for no fucking reason, I'm alive.

If you call seven years of prison living.

# 1

*Nine years later…*
*Dax*

**My damaged hog rattles** between my thighs. Add the hot pavement rising up to sizzle the lower half of my body and the sun cooking my shoulders and I fucking guarantee it's hotter than hell.

If I manage to survive the next few hours, I'll need to repair my bike, which will be costly. That's really the least of my worries right now, and I shake off those thoughts. I should feel some form of redemption for saving the little girl who I just placed in safe arms. Kiley never deserved the drugged out mother who gave her life or what Fox, the president of the Desert Crows MC, had planned for her. The uncaring fog that's been with me for almost ten years cleared when I looked into Kiley's eyes. I didn't think my plan to remove Kiley from the house would succeed, and I expected to die. Sadly, Kiley would have died too, but death was better than the alternative. I made it out alive with the help of unlikely friends and now Kiley has a chance. The truth—it will take much more than one small child to save me after the shit I've done since leaving prison. Torture and murder are only half the story. If hell exists, there's an inferno waiting for me.

I swerve around a pothole on the blacktop. In less than fifteen minutes, all hell will break loose. I survived seven years in prison, but my chances of surviving what's next are about nil. The men riding behind me know what we're heading into and, like me, they're ready to die.

We're ex-cons and we've drawn our line between the wrong we're willing to live with and the wrong we can't abide by. Fox making plans to sell Kiley to a child molester was the line we drew in the hot desert sand. The Desert Crows MC is made up of ex-cons like us. I have no idea who will have my back and who won't. One thing I do know—I'm not going back to prison or standing by and allowing Fox to continue his shit.

The Desert Crows' clubhouse is a mile off Highway 87 in Peach City, Arizona, an hour northeast of Phoenix. Around a thousand people call Peach City home, and the area is sparse with a temperature about five degrees lower than Phoenix, which means it's still damn hot.

The dusty dirt road leading up to the club is shit on a Harley and makes cleaning the filters regularly a must. We thump along over the ruts until the twelve inch wood posts supporting an iron script sign with the club's name comes into view. I stop and idle as the other four bikes pull up beside me.

"Last chance to turn around," I tell Skull, Johns, Coke, and Vampire. My supporters. The men who are as fed up as I am.

Skull brushes his fingers over his bald head before revving his engine. "We're with you, Dagger," he says when the noise fades. Dagger is my club name. "I think Loki and Bear will side with you too. Try not to shoot them," he adds.

"Got it," I say and hope I can avoid doing just that. I look at them. Ex-cons trying to find a place just like I am. Sadly, the place we all found is run by a piece of shit who is blood-thirsty, mean, and insane. Fox needs to die.

My wrist throbs. The damn thing is broken because the enforcer for Arizona's largest crime syndicate had me forced off the road. It's also the reason my bike is damaged. I wasn't happy about any of that, but a little girl is safe because those same people helped me. If I survive, I won't forget what I owe them. I unstrap the Velcro from the wrist support they gave me in the emergency room and toss it into the dirt.

No weakness.

I rev my engine and lead the way. We pass beneath the iron sign and keep going. The clubhouse sits about a hundred feet back from the fenced entrance. The building is a clapboard mess covered here and there with extra sheets of plywood. The roof is rusted tin and echoes like a motherfucker when it rains, which thankfully isn't often. The place should have been condemned years ago. Rusted out vehicles and bikes are scattered around the yard and mixed with household garbage. No dignity whatsoever, just piles of crap. I'll admit most of our members drive rat bikes made of a lot of shit from the yard. I'm tired of it. We all know Fox stashes a good portion of money without sharing with the brothers. That and the pigsty out here will change if I survive.

It's strange that saving Kiley gave me back part of the man I was before Savannah died. The other part died with her and our son. I'm not sure about the new me. I just know I want change for this club or I want to send it to hell.

Fox has connections with the county or he intimidates them, so planning and zoning leave us alone. I'm not privy to those connections. The locals aren't fond of the club, but they give us exactly what we want—privacy to run our illegal operations. The way I figure it, Fox also gets tips on pending raids. It's uncanny how he always knows. It's part of the way he controls us. We're in the dark, and most of the men, including me, thought of Fox as a savior until a short time ago. No one in the club wants to return to prison and no matter that we break just about every law there is, Fox keeps prison at bay.

I clear my mind of everything but the coming confrontation. I park and lift my leg over the seat. I leave my gun holstered at the back of my waist. I'm known for using a blade and I prefer it. I'm not beyond shooting Fox if it comes down to him or me. There are rules for what's about to go down. That doesn't mean Fox will follow them.

With the four guys at my back, I open the front door of the clubhouse. It makes an obnoxious squeak as it swings wide and slams against the wall. I look across the warm, shadowed interior and see Fox sitting on a bar stool. He turns slowly when Rufus, our only prospect, who is tending the bar, freezes. Fox stands slowly. He's not stupid and knows something is going down. Skull was on guard duty today watching Kiley and so was Metal. Metal isn't with us because I cut his throat to save the child. His blood is still splattered across the front of my leather cut that displays the Desert Crow colors on the back. I'll wash it off if I survive.

Fox spits to the side and hikes his jeans up an inch. His gun rests at his hip. It's an easier draw for him than mine is for me. Fox stands five ten and he's thick without carrying excess fat. He keeps himself in shape. He's wearing a black T-shirt I've seen many times. The front reads, "Mouths don't get pregnant." His oily scalp, deeply inset eyes, and flat nose give him the look of an inbred shit for brains. I don't let it fool me because Fox didn't get where he is by being stupid. He's a crazy mother and has no fear of death and no problem walking up to someone holding a gun on him until the barrel is pushed against his forehead. I saw him do it once. He stabbed the guy without caring that the man's finger rested on the gun's trigger. Like I said, he's crazy.

I keep my hands at my side. The charter rules say I can challenge. Those rules go back thirty-five years to when Fox was a toddler and I wasn't even a thought to the parents who raised me. This doesn't mean Fox won't kill me before I challenge.

"Well, well, fucker. You finally grew a set, because there's no way you would take Skull away from his duty if this was a Sunday school lesson." Fox looks me up and down before his steely blue eyes hit the guys behind me. I have no idea if they're meeting his gaze in challenge or planning to stab me in the back. I'm risking everything on the former.

Two club members rise from chairs at a table to my right. Clutch has his perpetual unlit cigarette hanging from his lips. He's one of the few members with shaggy hair. It's naturally bleach blond, so Fox lets it slide. Clutch is Fox's VP combined with Sergeant at Arms, and I may need to go through him to get to Fox. Is Fox in the mood to kill me himself? That's the million-dollar question.

Clutch moves closer to Fox without taking his gaze from me. Loki is the other guy who stood from the table. He's the exact opposite of Fox when it comes to muscle. His bulk is fat and he has a lot of it. He moves slowly. His plus is that very little in the way of physical damage affects him. The fat just jiggles with each punch. I was in a bar fight with him once and three guys attacked him and couldn't take him down. Right now, he stands still. I watch his eyes shift to someone behind me and I hope it's a good sign.

Red, Fox's retired whore, backs away to the far corner of the room. She's somewhere in her forties but looks older. She's been around longer than most of the members. That fact gives testament that she's dangerous even though she doesn't look it. I've fucked a few of the whores at the clubhouse, but she's not one of them. She managed to kick her meth habit years ago, and I have no idea why she stays in this shit place. She keeps the other whores in line and rules the pussy roost. I consider her in Fox's back pocket. For some reason, he treats her better than he does the other women.

Very slowly I remove the knife from the sheath at my waist. Once it's free, I jam it down on the wooden table beside me. I look around at the silent men and then settle my eyes back on Fox. "I challenge for the club." This leaves no doubt that I want Fox dead.

Things are about to get fuck-all ugly.

# 2

*Sofia*

**Her bare fist skims** my jaw without causing damage. The woman in the ring with me hasn't been that lucky. I lost my last fight and have no intention of going down again. I kick my leg out and she moves to the side. Her mistake is dropping her right arm. I take advantage and let my fist fly. The solid blow sends her to the sand. There are no refs and I take advantage of that while she's down by kicking her in the head and chest.

This is street fighting, though here in Florida we do it on the beach. The people watching and placing bets form the ring. Nothing glamorous about the fight itself or the payout.

Whoever the girl is, she doesn't get up. She tries to crawl away and I won't have that. I lean down, grab her ponytail, lift her head, and kick her full in the face. It finishes her and cheers and groans swell from the crowd. Joey Jay, promotor, trainer, and all-around piece of shit, walks over and throws his arm around my shoulder. I shrug him off and grab the water bottle from his other hand. I tip it back and allow the water to wash the sweat and splattered blood from my face before taking a drink.

"Ya did it, girl. I knew you weren't down after that last fight. You got your mojo back."

He looks so pleased with himself. It's not him who takes the abuse. I'm fucking twenty-six years old, barely make a living, and have the shit kicked out of me on a regular basis. No more. This was my last fight. I have bigger fish to fry.

"Fuck you, Joey. I said I was done and I meant it. My ass is out of this city. Get me the money and don't take any detours."

"Sofia, ya did it. You're on a roll—"

I cut him off. "I lost the last fight, shit for brains. Winning this one does not make it a roll. Get my money, lose my number, and pray I never see you again, fuck wad."

He shakes his head, kicks some sand, and walks away to find the money man. He doesn't believe me. It's okay, though. I have a throwaway phone in my car with one phone number in it. That number does not belong to Joey. I'll be long gone before his ass wakes up in the morning.

I'm on a mission and the chances are good I will never return to Pensacola. Not because the place is so bad. If I had a normal job, it might even be a great place to live. The problem, I can't work at anything remotely normal. I have anger issues with a huge chip on my shoulder. Fighting is the only way to relieve the pressure that swells inside of me and turns me into a crazy bitch. It's one of the reasons I'm leaving.

I have an appointment with destiny.

I'm heading to Arizona and the small town of Peach City. My mother called it *el diablo*. She swore she would never return. It's one of the few promises she kept before she died. I have a score to settle because of the man who destroyed my mother's life. I've put it off long enough. I'm going there to kill him. My mom lived in fear every minute of every day even though she escaped to the other side of the country. For as long as I remember, I've dreamed of killing Frank Tison. The only fear I've ever carried is the thought that someone got to him first.

My mother crossed the Arizona-Mexico border as a child. Several people in her group died making the journey, including one of her aunts. She said they spent days in the back of a van with the sun beating down on the metal and turning the interior into a hot tin can—no ventilation and very little air with temperatures over a hundred degrees. They had warm water, which is the only thing that saved the eight illegals who made it out alive.

My grandparents survived the crossing, lived a few more years, then died long before I was born. My mother had no one. She was here in the United States illegally and worked multiple, low-paying jobs to stay off the street. She met Frank Tison when he pulled up on his motorcycle where she was emptying trash from one of the homes she cleaned. He asked her if she wanted a ride. I can only imagine how my mother looked at that age. I've been called beautiful—large brown eyes with the corners pulled down slightly, long dark hair, and olive skin give me an exotic look. My mother was proud of her Tzeltal Maya origin. They are strong and resilient people, she often told me. The Mexican government forced her family, along with the community, from their homes in the rainforest in 1971. My mother was six years old and remembers relatives, especially the young children, starving to death after the evacuation. Coming to the United States was a blessing for those who survived the crossing.

She didn't take the ride on Frank's bike that day, but he was persistent, and within a few weeks, he won her over. In just a few months, he had her addicted to drugs and prostituted her out to his friends and associates. My mother cried the first time she told me the story. I just wanted to beat the shit out of someone. Yes, Frank was my first choice but anyone would do. My mother was high as a kite and most likely never remembered telling me about my father that first time. I was seven years old.

Through the years, always when she was high, she'd tell me more. Frank nearly killed her twice when he discovered she was pregnant. Both times she lost the baby. When she was used up and old beyond her years, Frank's friends lost interest. To remain in his environment, she crawled on her hands and knees to serve Frank so he would keep her supplied with drugs. She did this until she discovered she was pregnant again, with me. The only child she was sure was Frank's. She hid the pregnancy and managed to escape before I was born. An advocacy center took her in and helped her get off drugs.

When I was a year old, a woman who helped my mother stay clean was caring for me when Frank caught my mother leaving a store. He beat her so badly she almost died and was hospitalized for weeks. He did it in plain sight of the public, in the parking lot where he discovered her. No one stopped him.

By that time, with the help of the advocacy center, my mother had her citizenship. The judge sentenced Frank to five years in prison. Sadly, the so-called hard sentence was because of his priors. Frank swore he would search down my mother and kill her and me. He didn't care that the judge heard him threaten us. My mom believed him and left everything behind to keep me safe. Her battle with drugs wasn't over, though. She'd stay clean for six months to a year and then fall off the wagon again. Child services took me away more times than I can count. I would be shuffled off to family after family who wanted me for the added money. When I grew older, foster parents couldn't handle my boat load of problems. It always ended in being dumped back with my mom and all her fucking promises.

I wasn't an easy child to deal with and I never graduated high school. I was kicked out of almost every school I attended until I was sixteen and talked my mom into signing the paperwork so I wouldn't need to go back.

Socially, my fists did the talking. Look at me wrong and I'd kick your ass. Or at least sometimes. Depending on who I went up against, my ass was also kicked. I didn't care if you were male or female, big or small, I'd try to take you down for as little as a sideways look.

I blame my issues first on Frank and then on my mom. Anger replaced the babies that Frank killed. Anger is my closest relative now. A year ago, I found my mother dead with a syringe injected in her arm. I had no money to bury her, so the state handled it. After her death, I went on a fighting rampage and proved that taking a punch is my specialty. The rampage lasted until the fight before this one. I should have died and it's taken me almost two months to get back on my feet and ready to fight again. I'm only here because I needed money to make my trip across the country.

Revenge is the only thing that keeps me going.

The worst part and the reason I can't forgive my mother is all the drugged-out ramblings I listened to through the years. She still loved the son of a bitch and forgave him for killing my sister and brother. That's who they are in my head—an unborn boy and a girl. I'd have a family if not for Frank, and he'll pay for what he did. My quest will either end my life or allow me to live on something besides violence. It's fed my soul for far too long.

When I finally hold Frank's severed dick in my hands, maybe I, Sofia Guadalupe Acosta, can finally be happy.

# 3

*Dax*

**Fox laughs. It's a** low, throaty sound that rises from deep in his chest. He's so pompous and I want nothing more than to wipe the smile off his face. Hell, I want to take the smile and cram it down his throat, push it past his belly, and down farther until it shoots from his ass. My body twitches with the need to attack.

His smile flips to a scowl. "You think you can take me, kid?"

I pull the knife from the table and slide it back in its sheath. "I'm counting on it," I say between teeth clenched so hard my jaw aches.

Fox takes his eyes off me like my challenge is nothing. "What d'ya think, Clutch?"

Clutch doesn't smile, ever. "Shoot 'em and clean the floor with his body. You boys behind Dagger got a death wish too?" Clutch asks.

Skull takes a step to my left side. "A challenge has been made. Which one of you wants to put in your tampon and accept it?"

My lips twitch. Skull always has a quick wit. He's also a mean fucker when he needs to be. I'm glad he's on my side.

Fox nods at Skull. "Fuck you. Clutch can deal with you, I'll handle the kid."

Fox is the only member who never calls me by my club nickname or my real name. He's called me "kid" since I met him in prison. I think it's because he knew it bothered me back then. I was a twenty-year-old kid and had trouble hiding my feelings. It was a dangerous habit and the first forty-eight hours behind prison bars cured me of it.

"Fists," Fox says with a look of glee. "I'm gonna beat the shit out of ya, kid, and make sure I teach everyone in this club not to fuck with me. You woulda been smart to stab me in the back when I wasn't lookin'. The mistake will cost you your hell-bound soul." Fox spits on the floor between us.

My broken wrist will be a problem. With knives, I had a chance. So be it. "I don't have a soul, Fox. You should know that by now." I shrug out of my cut and then pull my T-shirt over my head. I also slip out the two knives in my boots and lay them on my cut, which I've placed on the table that I sank the knife blade into. Next is the gun. The brothers push tables aside for the fight. While they do, I quiet my brain and focus my attention completely on Fox as he shrugs out of his cut and relieves himself of his weapons. I have height on Fox but not much else. I've seen him demolish men twice his size. He's a mean motherfucker and has no off button.

The men form a circle and whispers from behind me chant, "Desert Crows forever, forever Desert Crows." I charge forward leading with my shoulder. Fox tries to sidestep, but I planned on that and turn with him and ram him hard. My weight takes him back a foot but that's about it. I didn't even manage to knock the breath out of him. His fist hits the side of my head and I stagger back. That's when another sledgehammer fist takes me in the jaw and I see stars. Four men came with me today and because of me, they will die. At least I'll die knowing Kiley is safe. But the truth is… for the first time since Savannah and my son were murdered, I don't want to die.

I twist and avoid another shot to my head and manage to land a solid blow to Fox's chest. Using my injured left wrist, I tighten my fist and let it fly. The crunch of Fox's nose isn't sweet enough to deactivate the pain ringing up my arm. I imagine dying hurts more. Fox puts me in a bear hug to stop another punch and squeezes me. It hurts. Blood heats my face as I'm deprived of oxygen. Fox turns me away from him and slips his arm up so it tightens around my throat. He lands repeated strikes to my ribcage with his left fist while squeezing my neck in an arm bar.

He's laughing when he tosses me down to the floor. "Fucking killing you is too easy. You need to suffer a little bit more, boy."

I've regressed from kid to boy, but I don't give a fuck. I'm just able to get my hands and feet beneath me when his boot lands in my side. Fuck it hurts. I cough and try to breathe. With my last reserves, I throw myself at his knees, wrap my arms around him, and push off the floor with my legs. Who needs to breathe?

I take Fox down and a table crashes beneath us. Another blow lands against my skull. My vision is black around the edges, but my wrist no longer hurts. I push myself out of the way of a knee landing in my throat and grab his other leg. Fox tries to roll but can't. He grabs a chair and brings it up and over himself striking me with it, busting the chair in pieces. I feel nothing. I release his leg and push the broken pieces off me. All but one. The leg of the chair is jagged.

The table that broke held my weapons. Fox goes for my gun, which is a foot from his right arm. I stab the wood into his leg and he grunts. I raise my arm again, gain leverage, and I sink the sharp wood into his side. I scramble up so I'm above Fox, who is now screaming. He rolls to his back to protect himself. It does no good. I bring my weapon down and plow the stake into his chest.

A gun explodes close to me. I expect pain. It's not me who goes down, though. Skull holds the smoking gun and it's Clutch who drops.

"Dagger might enjoy rolling across the floor, I don't." Skull says as he points his weapon around the room.

That's when I notice that several more club members have come in from the back. Hands go into the air. Vamp, Coke, and Johns have their guns out too. I'm covered in Fox's blood with Metal's blood beneath it. I lean over Fox's body and grab my gun while unsteadily rising to my feet.

"Fingers interlocked, hands on top of your head," I tell everyone in the room. I'm breathing heavily and fighting the pain that is now throbbing through my wrist and arm.

Red hasn't moved from her corner, and she's smiling ear to ear. So noted. Rufus, the prospect, went down for armed robbery as a young teenager and was tried as an adult. He served five years in state after three in juvie. He only got out a few months ago. Like the rest of us, he had nowhere to go, so he signed on with the Crows. He's wearing a slight grin and nods my way. Again, noted.

"Who has a problem with the new leadership?" I huff out still trying to catch my breath. No one moves. "This is your chance.

Walk out, take your bike, and never cross paths with Desert Crows again."

It takes a moment. Then, very slowly, one of the men who came into the clubhouse after the battle began removes his cut and tosses it to the floor. The ultimate disrespect to our colors. I step aside as he walks out.

"Anyone else?" I ask.

Curly Sue, one of the old-timers in the club, takes a step forward. Skull's gun turns on him. He lifts his hands higher. "Like most of us, I don't like the shit that's been going down. I'd rather ride free than see this club go even further into the shit. I'd like to hear your plans before I make a decision."

This is better than I expected. If all hell doesn't break loose after what I have to say, we might have a chance. "Anyone else feel that way?" Three others agree with Curly, including Loki. "Call everyone into the table. If they come with guns blazing, they're as dead as Fox and Clutch. Anyone who chooses to leave when I'm done speaking has a one-time pass."

Curly Sue nods and takes out his phone.

"Put your gun away," I tell Skull. He gives me a stern look before doing as I say. I glance over my shoulder and eye the three men behind me before giving them a nod. They holster their weapons too.

Everyone's attention turns to Red as she walks toward us. She stops in front of Fox's body and spits on him. She looks up at me and grins. "Had it comin' for a long time. I'll continue handling the girls if you don't mind. That is, if I like what you have to say."

Whores, or any woman for that matter, don't attend church or as I just called it—the table. "This once. If you want to bring the whores in, do it. They'll also have free passage to leave if they chose to."

"Won't be leaving. They need the white crunch too badly."

This isn't the time to tell her we are going out of the meth business. I want everyone here when I explain the cold, hard truth about the new leadership. I grab Fox's cut and using my knife remove the president's patch. I jam it in my pants' pocket. The Desert Crows as it was under Fox, the illegal business dealings, and the skinhead mentality are at an end.

# 4

*Sofia*

**Driving gives me plenty** of time to think. You could say my life passes before my eyes. I've carried so much anger for so long that I don't even know what to do to stop it other than kill Frank. What then? I keep asking myself as my car eats up the miles between me and revenge. I stay on the road for twelve hours before pulling into a cheap but clean hotel and calling it a night. Now I'm lying in bed and asking the same question.

My room is on the bottom floor and loud, stomping footsteps ring overhead every ten minutes or so and I can't sleep. I should be exhausted. I'll be in Peach City the day after tomorrow. I could have done the seventeen hundred miles in two days, but I want to be at my best when I confront the man who's caused so much heartache in my life. I'll stay the night in western New Mexico before I reach the border into Arizona. If tomorrow night goes anything like tonight, I should just drive straight through and get the job done. I roll over with the pillow over my head.

I toss and turn for hours, and sometime after two in the morning, I sleep. I wake up feeling groggy and decide to take a jog to try to shake the heaviness out of my body. I stay in good shape to fight and earn money. I plan to shoot Frank with my Smith and Wesson .38 Special. Five shots that pack a punch. The gun is small and easy to conceal. If I can't kill Frank in five shots, it's because I'm already dead. Really though, I want to beat him to death and listen to him beg while I break every bone in his body.

I take off out the front door of the hotel. It's in an industrial area and most likely not the safest place for a woman to run early in the morning. It would be sweet if someone challenged me. The muscles in my legs ripple as I slide along the pavement. Unfortunately, no one bothers me. I guess I don't look like an easy mark. If anything, I look like the Latina hood-girl I am.

I hit the shower after returning to the room. When I'm ready to go, I carry my bag out to the car and step inside the hotel lobby for the free continental breakfast. It's decent and the coffee is hot and black, which is what I really need. I take an apple and banana to eat in the car and continue on my way.

I think about Frank again. What will he look like? Will I recognize him by some small tell I see in the mirror each day? My mother says I look nothing like him. I hope she's right. We'll see.

The miles tick by. I stop at a fast-food junk house, use the restroom, and order lunch. I place the bag in my lap and drive. I try to eat healthy when I have enough money for decent food, but the last thing I'm thinking about right now is the condition of my arteries in twenty years.

I hit New Mexico in the afternoon. It's not what I would call a pretty state, at least not the part I'm driving through, which is close to the Mexico border. I slow down when I enter a small dustbowl town and creep through at twenty-five miles an hour as the speed sign dictates.

I'm sleepy, and a few hours ago, a sense of melancholy descended. It happens from time to time. It's another reason I fight. When you're someone like me, there's nowhere to go for depression. Hell, I don't need some fucking head shrink to call a spade a spade. My wiring is fucked up and fighting cures all my evils.

A burnt-orange, stuccoed Catholic church sits about twenty feet back from the road. The building is old and beside it is a field with large wooden crosses spaced about twenty feet apart. There are four crosses on two sides with two crosses at either end. It's the name of the church that makes me turn around. Our Lady of Guadeloupe Mission is spelled out in script letters above the door. Guadalupe is my middle name, though spelled differently from the sign. For some strange reason, the church beckons me.

My mother was Catholic, and when she wasn't high, she took comfort in the never-changing ceremony of her religion. As soon as I was old enough to make my opinions known, I refused to go. I think that was around the time I was seven or eight and the state awarded me back to my mom.

The mission is nothing like the Catholic churches in the Florida area where I'm from. This one is built in the Spanish style. The front arched entrance is also a bell tower. There are two arched stained-glass windows to either side of the entry. I park and step from my beat-up car that I can barely afford. My feet steer me on a course I never thought to travel.

The humidity of Florida is far behind me. It's hot and dry as I walk through the arched entry and place my hand on the old metal door lever. I push it down with my thumb and pull back. The old wooden door opens with a loud groan.

The interior is cool and welcoming. A strange sense of serenity spreads through me. The door slowly shuts and the mission is quiet… peaceful. I stand quietly and look around. I see no one. There's one center aisle with eight wooden pews to either side. I move forward past the holy water and stop when I'm standing in front of the Virgin Mary—her arms spread wide in welcome. Above is her son hanging from the cross. I notice a few lit candles on an altar to the side. Someone must be here, but they don't make their presence known.

I look around again and inhale deeply. I remember this smell from my childhood—incense. My mother only took me to church when she wasn't drugged out. Why couldn't she beat her demons? Why did she love a horrible man who abused her? No one answers my questions—not the Virgin Mary or Jesus. I don't fucking cry, and it makes me angry that pressure builds behind my eyes. I feel a presence and look around, ready to run out the door. I see no one. I scream and the sound echoes throughout the small building. No one comes running to see the crazy woman standing at the front of the church having a breakdown. "God," I say aloud. It's not blasphemy, it's a request for help. I can't take the anger, the loneliness, the pain any longer. I sink to my knees. Everything wrong with my life swells in a rush of emotion. When I was very young, I had dreams. I laughed. I played. My childhood was stolen. Anger, resentment, and revenge eat me alive.

I look up at the statue before me. Is it wrong to want more? Want someone to love who loves me in return? I remember having a rag doll when I was small. I cherished her. Is it normal to stop loving and allow hatred to fill you so you can make it through each day?

Never enough food. Secondhand, threadbare clothing. No electricity or water at times. What is so wrong with me that as a child I was punished this way?

The tears finally come. Tears I've hidden away inside me for years. I cry for who I could have been. I cry for the babies, the siblings I never knew. I have no idea how long I stay on my knees. I finally wipe my eyes and rise. The candles, like the church, call me. I take one and light two more. They represent my unborn brother and sister. My fingers tremble as I light one more. It's for my mother. I hope now she's free of her demons. I should light one for myself and ask forgiveness for my sins.

I don't. Standing here brings me to terms with my death.

I will kill Frank Tison and the Desert Crows will kill me. I turn and walk outside. The sun is beginning to set and tomorrow will be here soon enough.

My future sin is unforgivable.

# 5

*Dax*

**Including six women and** one prospect, there are twenty-two of us. Two members didn't show. A side room off the main area has a table where the club officers usually meet. It won't hold everyone we have here tonight, so we're set up in the main room. The men are restless and the women appear their normal strung-out mess if you don't count Red. The women start at around twenty years old. There have been younger ones, but it was bringing heat to the club, so Fox started sneaking the young ones in for gangbangs. They were anywhere from sixteen and up and he'd hand them drugs and send them on their way when the brothers were through with them. That's never been my scene. I like fucking women, grown women. But, I stood by knowing it was happening and that makes me just as guilty.

Fuck, this needs to work. I can no longer travel the path of the man I was.

We've pulled the tables into a loose circle on the main floor of the clubhouse. The only cool air we have comes from an old evap-cooler, which barely handles the sweltering temperature. A creaking ceiling fan circulates the air and helps a little. Half the members are seated and half are standing. The women wait beside the pool table, which is as far away from the meeting area as they can get. I look at them. All but Red is skeletal thin with sores on their arms and faces.

I know some of the brothers use on occasion even though Fox discouraged it. As far as I'm concerned he never gave a shit about his brothers. For him it was a money issue. And using up the drugs before selling them hit Fox in the wallet. Total bullshit because members saw little if any of the money earned from drug sales. Fox was money-stingy with the men and drug-stingy with the whores. He kept all of us needy, not just the women.

What the hell am I doing? I ask myself for the hundredth time. Most of the current brothers were with me when we killed two members of a black street gang. They had killed one of our whores, or so we thought. We handed down retribution like we gave a fuck about the women, which wasn't true. The men's deaths were nasty and I still remember their screams. Hell their screams have woken me from sleep more times than I care to count. Skinning them alive is why Fox trusted me with Kiley. Metal and Clutch helped. Even so the deaths are on me. It earned me a reaper patch and nightmares. Fox later told me, while ranting drunkenly, that he killed the woman and let those two men take the blame. What did I do? Again, nothing. I kept my mouth shut and tried like hell to forget it happened. For years I stayed buried in my grief and anger without letting go. That shit is over and my actions from here forward will define who I want to be.

Some of these men won't like it. I will set this club on a better path, though.

To gain everyone's attention, I stand and gaze around the room. Slowly, the talking dies down. I pause a bit longer before speaking. "We have a lot to discuss," I finally say. "I'll give you the rundown of a few changes that start immediately." Skull, Vamp, Coke, and Johns are on board with me, so at least I have their backing. "After you hear the new rules, those who want the hell out can leave. If you go, you will remove your colors and no longer be a Desert Crow. Or be welcomed back. Your decision to leave is final." I remain standing. "All members take a seat." Half the men nod, several keep their scowling faces on me without blinking, and several look away. Each man takes a seat, though. I need to get the first item out in the open and get rid of a few undecideds before I lay all my cards on the table. "My challenge to Fox was a long time coming. I put up with shit I'm not proud of. Taking the child, Kiley, was the last straw. No one in this room should hold with a child molester, and Fox planned to sell her to the highest bidding fucking cho-mo he could find." I see movement in the corner where the women are and notice Kiley's mother, Pauline, take a step away from the women. She's glaring at me.

Tough shit.

"I had to ask for help to rescue Kiley and now our club owes a debt," I continue as I give a hard stare-down to some of the angry eyes cast my way. They don't need to know the entire story, but they need to know the who. "Moon's organization helped me."

The silence that follows this statement lasts all of five seconds. Oho, who has remained fairly quiet, leaps to his feet. "That's fuckin' bullshit. I don't owe no debt to some wetback spics." Grumbles in the room increase while Oho clenches and unclenches his fists. His face and bald head are bright red.

I keep calm on the outside. "You're right, Oho, you don't owe the debt, the club does. The fucking door is waiting for you. And if some small piece of lint in your head urges you to stick around, I would suggest you disregard it." I finger the knife sheath at my hip.

Oho shoves the table in front of him forward and it crashes on its side. Johns and Vampire make a grab for him. I strategically placed those who are loyal to me in between those I question. I knew Oho was the biggest threat. Johns and Vampire are ready for his bullshit. They slam him face first to the floor. He continues cussing until he runs out of steam. I nod at Johns and Vampire when he stops fighting and they lift him up. There's blood running down his face.

"Lay down your colors," I tell him.

Oho stares around the circle at the other members. "You really takin' this shit? Next thing you know, he'll be dealing with niggers."

I knew this would be ugly. I look Oho straight in the eyes and try to keep my temper in check. "You're wrong about that," I tell him. "I won't be dealing with the likes of you. Anyone who can help pull this club out of the pile of dog shit it's been rolling in has a chance. I don't give a fuck what color their skin is. You would have killed that baby's aunt and allowed Kiley to go to a cho-mo. The only nigger I'm looking at is you and that includes anyone who wants to side with you."

I look around again. "If you do, get the fuck out now." All attention is back on me. "If you plan to stay, you need to know a few facts about exactly who we are. It's time we begin living up to our name." I take my cut off and turn it around so everyone sees the emblem. "We're Crows—a tight-knit family. Loyal. We protect our territory. Like a crow, we're fucking smart and use whatever tool at hand makes life easier. We hold a grudge and never forget a face.

Desert crows are scrappier than most. They... we, need to be in order to live in this environment. This club has forgotten everything our name stands for. It's our legacy and we need to take it back. Now ask yourself what our colors stand for because every fucking crow I've ever seen in my life is black. You want to be a racist, fine, but you sure as hell better pick a name for your club other than Desert Crows. I don't give a fuck what color a crow is. I want to be proud wearing these colors and I want to be a part of a club with the same fucking values as our namesake." The vest rests against my chest and I strike my palm against it. "You want to be a bigoted SOB, fine, become a pussy-ass white dove for all I care."

There it is... my Hail Mary. I shrug back into my vest. It's time to see how the dust settles.

Without looking at me, one of the newer members, Candy, with a fucking swastika tattooed on his bare scalp, removes his cut and rests it on the table. He walks over to Oho and waits. Oho removes his vest and tosses it to the floor before spitting on it. He shoves Vampire aside and the two men walk out. Vampire follows and watches them through the open door. All the brothers are on their feet by this time. I take my seat again and wait for everyone but Vampire to do the same. With a nod from me, he knows to stay where he is and guard the door.

My eyes travel the room while I talk. "Each man here served time. Inside, you lived by those fucked up race rules because you had no choice. We are no longer in the hellhole they call state prison and by-damned we're going to stop acting like it. Fox kept us isolated because he never wanted anyone thinking past survival. You are no longer under Fox or his henchmen's thumb. I won't live by or lead by those rules."

I inhale deeply and gather myself again. My heart is pounding against my chest like I've run for miles. "That doesn't mean we're turning pussy-whipped. We have a chance to build this club into something that works for everyone. Meth and other illegal drugs are not the answer." I pause a moment to let that sink in. The women begin muttering quietly and Pauline looks over her shoulder at them with what I assume is an, *I told you so* expression. I ignore her and continue. "No one here is an idiot. You know Fox was fucking you over with his own agenda. Some of you have old ladies and families. Are they better off since leaving prison?" I pound my fist on the table in frustration over how we've lived. "I sure as fuck am not. And I'm not proud of some of the shit I've done." My hand goes flat as I try to reel in my emotions. "We may still be required to do shit we aren't proud of, but I say we take a vote on the big items and stop having one person make decisions for us while treating us like a bunch of fucked up shitheads. We need to clean this mess up. It's time for you to make a choice. It's the last chance you'll have…" I wave toward the front door, "to walk safely away with no repercussions."

"What the fuck are we supposed to do?" All heads turn to Pauline. The guys refer to her as *Powder* because she'll do anything for a hit of meth. She may have been pretty at one time, but drugs have turned her into a skeletal caricature of a woman. The sores covering her arms and face kept me away from what's between her legs and I never understood why any of the men took what she offered. If it wasn't for her treatment of Kiley, I might feel sorry for her.

I push back from the table a bit and turn my full attention to the women. "Most of you are addicts." That's an understatement because I'd bet my ass, except for Red, they all are. "That won't work here anymore. You get clean or get out." The next part is rough but the truth. "Club whores are a dime a dozen. If you clean up and want to keep spreading your legs, that's fine, you have a place to do it within this club."

When I finish laying out these rules, Pauline explodes. Red tries to grab her as she runs toward me with fists flying. I stand and bring my palm up, striking her chest dead center and shoving her backward as hard as I can. With all the bad shit I've done, hitting a woman wasn't on the list until now. Pauline flies back and lands on her ass. She wraps her arms across her chest while trying to catch her breath. "That was for Kiley," I grind out. "Any mother who would stand by and watch her child sold isn't welcome here. Pick your sorry ass up and get the fuck out."

She starts muttering as she rolls to her knees. I only catch part of what she says, but it's enough to make me cross the several feet separating us and grab her by a chunk of hair. I lift her head, painfully arching her neck back. "What did you say?"

She's furious, her eyes filled with hatred. Fear too, which shouldn't satisfy me as much as it does. She's stupid to challenge me right now. "You don't know shit. Fox hid the money and you have no idea where. Fuck you." She tries to scramble away, but I hold on.

We all knew there was money, most likely a shitload. Very slowly, I slip my knife from its sheath. I release Pauline's hair and place my arm around her throat, pulling her up from the floor with her back to me. I lift the knife and she starts screaming, making a high-pitched animal-type sound.

"Shh," I tell her and tighten my hold to keep her from wiggling free. She makes a gargling sound as she struggles for air. "You can start talking or I can start by removing your ear." I loosen my hold just enough for her to breathe and then I touch the tip of the knife to her skin. She freezes. "Count of three and the bottom half comes off." The last thing I planned to do was mess with one of the women. I'm making my stand, though, and each man and woman here needs to know I'm not fucking around.

"No need to cut her. I know where it is," Red says as she steps forward.

I lift my eyes from Pauline. Red appears worried and I never realized how soft-hearted she was. "Good, if she doesn't talk, I'll kill her and can get what I need from you." Will I? It's easy to say and quite another thing to follow through on. I'm not Fox. Pauline continues crying. I keep my eyes on Red. "One."

"You asshole," Pauline says between sobs. "In his room, he hides it under the boards below the window."

I ease back the knife and glance at Skull. "Go check the room." I toss Pauline aside and she goes to her knees. I walk back to the table and glance at the men. They appear angry. I doubt it's over the fact I threatened to kill Pauline. More likely it's that at least two of the women were in on Fox's stash of money and we weren't. Typical Fox. Too bad I already killed the prick.

A few minutes later, Skull comes back carrying a large leather saddlebag. He drops it on the table. I unbuckle it and empty the contents.

Fuck me.

Bundles of hundred dollar bills scatter. I remove a rubber band and count one bundle. "Ten thousand," I say aloud when I'm finished. I stack the bundles on the table. There are thirty-two total. Coke whistles.

"That's our money," says AJ, one of the men who had Fox's back. I'm surprised he didn't leave with Oho. He's in his thirties, bushy beard, bald head, and green eyes. He's not the biggest guy we have, but no one would call him small. He's quiet and has an old lady, and I often wondered what the hell he's doing here. He followed Fox's dictates without grumbling. Questioning Fox got you dead real quick and each man here knew it. Didn't mean you couldn't tell when someone didn't like something. AJ was different. He did what Fox asked with more of a blank look than anything else.

I stare at AJ for a moment before answering. He doesn't shift his eyes away like he did earlier. "It's club money. Who the hell knows what Fox planned to do with it. The Crows have existed on selling drugs for too long. When you have no business to launder the money, that money is safer in bags." I know I'm defending Fox in a way, but I have a point to make. "This is only one of the problems I want brought to the table."

I need to take care of Pauline before we finish this conversation. "Skull, take Pauline to the small room." It's little more than a large closet with a lock on the outside of the door.

"Fuck you," Pauline screams as Skull makes a grab for her.

"I'll have one of the men give you a ride to the Valley when our meeting is over. If you wanna fight it, your ass can go out on the highway right now. You're done here. If you go to the cops, you're dead. This is the only free pass you'll get from this club." I notice two of the women crying. Red has her arms around them. The other woman, who answers to Tramp, is the youngest. The drugs haven't fucked up her looks too badly yet. Her hair is stringy and unwashed, and her face thin, but it's nothing like Pauline's. Her brown eyes hold intelligence when she isn't high. I've tapped her more than once. She's loud when she comes and disappears quickly when I'm finished. She's not a clinger and that's why I've gone back for more. Maybe she'll have a chance. "If you're leaving with Pauline, follow her and Skull to the small room. This part of the meeting is no longer your concern."

Red whispers to the two women she's holding. They both shake their heads. I glance at Tramp and she shakes her head too. The women live in an old trailer behind the clubhouse. The fucking trailer is a worse place to live than the clubhouse—hotter in the summer and colder in the winter. They need better accommodations. I tuck this thought away for later. Too much shit to handle right now. We'll see how the women come through withdrawals before tackling smaller problems.

Skull hauls Pauline over his shoulder. She screams the entire way to the small room. When they're out of sight, I lay down my plans. "Peach City has little to offer the four-wheeler and sand buggy enthusiasts who flock to the desert around here. They camp with their families and friends and bring a heavy need for gas and supplies. They tote their shit in, drive south to the reservation or north to Payson for those supplies. The club owns a chunk of property along the highway. Won't be cheap to get fuel tanks installed but a small store with essentials would be a good start. We have enough contractors in this room to make it happen within a few months." Up until today that's how I earned my living. "We also have bike mechanics. Four-wheelers and buggies aren't much different from motorcycles. When they break down, we can make money on repairs. I say we pull this club out of the dark side and get our shit together. I don't know about the rest of you but I'm tired of working for the man, driving to the Valley or Payson to do it, and making just enough money to put a roof over my head. Jobs aren't easy to come by for felons. I say we take it into our own hands."

AJ's chair squeaks as he pushes it back and stands. I expect him to lay down his cut. He jerks his chin at me. "I don't give a fucking fly's ass about the color of a man's skin as long as he's not dangerous to this club or my woman. I need work 'cause the old lady's having a baby. I like where you're going with this. What you got figured for officers now that Fox is dead?" This is not what I expected from AJ, but pending fatherhood does strange things to a man. I've been there.

"Congrats, brother." Coke slams him on the back and several others offer congratulations. I wait for the men to quiet. "Skull is my VP and Vampire Sergeant at Arms. Johns was an accountant before he got locked up in state, so he's taking over as treasurer. Didn't think we had any money for him to handle. Now he may have bitten off more than he can chew." The guys laugh. "Coke wants no part of voting rights, so I say my new officers step aside and let the brothers vote for who they want to sit regularly at the table."

Curly Sue, who's been mostly silent, speaks up. "AJ has my vote."

I look around and see a bunch of heads nod. AJ grunts. He backed Fox, but we all have respect for AJ. Unlike Fox's other henchmen, AJ stayed out of your business and never ratted if you said something about Fox. "Anyone else?" I ask.

No one volunteers another name. "Show of hands for AJ," I say.

All the men raise a hand.

For the first time today, I smile. "It looks like you're the new secretary, AJ."

"If my old lady doesn't kill me, I'll take the job," he says with a grin.

That's another thing I like about AJ...he has admitted to being pussy-whipped before and he has never cared about the hell the guys give him. A heavy feeling settles in my chest. I knew that feeling once too.

# 6

*Sofia*

**I stay the night** in a small Las Cruces hotel. It's clean, comfortable, and meets my needs.

I call Lorene, the only phone number in my new phone. She answers in a whisper. "Hey, can't talk right now, girlie. I'll call you back tomorrow." The call ends.

Lorene has no idea I'm coming for Frank. She's been part of the Desert Crows since Frank got my mother addicted to drugs. She also helped my mom escape. She's a strange one and the closest person I have as a friend. We've never met in person, but I know she would try to stop me if she knew my plans. I stare at the phone in my hand before resting it on the nightstand. I need sleep. I close my eyes and think of revenge. The statue of the Virgin Mary and the peace of the mission creep into my mind.

I'm tired. Tired of being angry. Tired of living a half-life and tired of hatred. I fall asleep cradled in the serenity from the church.

I sleep better than I expected and wake up easily. Today's the day. I should go for a run, but I decide on a large breakfast instead. There's a diner across the street from the hotel. After I shower, I walk over. Mountains surround Las Cruces. This is a far cry from the more tropical climate of Florida. It's just as hot, but low humidity makes it bearable.

I order a full meal. Maybe my last. I'm about four hundred miles from Peach City and I don't know if my stomach will be able to handle anything when I'm closer to my goal. The food has too much salt and they used canned vegetables for my omelet. The orange juice is concentrate. Even so, it's surprisingly edible. The coffee is good and strong, which helps too. I gaze out the window at the mountains. They're beautiful in their own way. If somehow I survive today and escape, could I build a home here?

I cut off the thought. It's too late for dreams.

The best I could hope for is prison. First degree murder is punishable by the death penalty in Arizona. I checked. So be it.

I toss three dollars on the table and walk out of the diner. I walk back across the street and jump in my car. I pull out of the parking lot and head to the nearest gas station to fill up. My money's running short and if I were staying in a hotel tonight, I wouldn't have enough. I jump on the highway and drive toward my destiny.

Daddy, here I come.

I turn off the radio and clear my head so it's as barren as the landscape and search for peace that won't come. Actual tumbleweeds roll beneath the tires as my car eats up the miles. I hit Phoenix a little after noon and stop for the restroom and more fuel.

I was right; my stomach can't handle food right now. I'm not nervous, but the closer I get, the more anticipatory adrenaline pumps through my veins. It's similar to how I feel before a fight. My phone rings after I finish filling the tank.

"Hey, lady," I say to Lorene in a bullshit, upbeat voice. I don't want anything to tip her off. I've figured out the general location of the clubhouse from talking to her through the years. I'm hoping she'll give me a heads up if Frank isn't there today. I just need to get the info in a roundabout way.

"That baby girl is safe and the shit's really hit the fan," she says. I won't deny it's a relief. I planned to call the cops before descending on the clubhouse and give them the information about the child they're holding. This makes things neater. "I have good news for you," Lorene continues. "You shouldn't tell someone over the phone that their father is dead, but I didn't think you'd mind hearing it. Dagger, one of the club members, is the new president. He killed the son of a bitch yesterday. He also got the baby to a safe place. There are some big changes coming."

"Dagger?" I say in shock. My heart is doing double-time and a knot is growing in the pit of my stomach.

"Yeh, he's about the nicest piece of man meat in these parts. Makes a woman stupid just lookin' at all those hot muscles. I've had my eye on him for a while now. Killed the man who killed his wife, stabbed him to death. Did his time and has been running with the Crows since. He didn't like the bullshit your daddy did with the club. That was sure as shit just from lookin' in his eyes. That man carries a lot of anger, reminds me of you sometimes. I'm telling ya, the club can only go up with him as prez." She gives a throaty laugh. "I need to go. I just wanted you to know that your old man is no longer breathin' air. Days like today are made for celebrating. Have a cold one for me."

She clicks off and I listen to dead air for a moment without pulling my phone away from my ear. My fingers tremble when I finally toss it in the seat next to me and grip the steering wheel. My vision goes dark around the edges. I breathe in and out and before I know it, I'm hyperventilating. The rage builds. It hasn't been this bad in a long time. "No," I scream into the car. This can't be happening. All these years of planning and my revenge is gone in one phone call. Gone when I'm finally within an hour of fulfilling my dream to destroy the man who caused so much pain.

I don't remember pulling out of the gas station and I'm barely aware of my surroundings. My phone gives directions and I mindlessly follow. Before I realize it, I'm heading out of Phoenix on Highway 87. I'm on autopilot and I need someone to suffer. Why? No one has a right to kill my father except me. No one!

Dagger… why the hell would he ruin my plans now? My rage carries me through the desert. I finally see the sign for Peach City. The name is a joke. The area is practically barren with only small shrubs and hills in the background. "Fucking Dagger," I murmur out loud.

I see the burned out property I've been looking for on the east side of the road. Lorene mentioned in one of her phone calls that it was a nostalgic junkyard of motorcycles and bicycles until it burned to the ground a few years ago. I turn onto the road directly past the blackened lot and travel about a mile. The pavement ends and I'm on dirt. I bounce around over potholes but don't consider slowing. My focus is on reaching the clubhouse.

I only slow to make the turn between double wood poles that signal I've found what I'm hunting for. Men are working in the yard dragging junk into a pile. The area is mostly clear and the stack of debris is huge. I stop the car and slide my gun from beneath the seat. Several of the men stop working and check me out. Keeping the gun in my lap, I remove it from the holster and slip it beneath the waistband of my jeans. I swing the car door open and step out into the boiling heat of the afternoon sun.

The mostly bald-headed men stand watching me—some with wife-beater T-shirts and some shirtless. They're scum. My father's scum. He owned these men, pulled them around by proverbial rings in their noses. "I'm here to see Dagger," I say loudly while stepping over a pile of motorcycle parts. I walk a few feet forward.

A man working more to the side of the building drops a shovel and strolls my way. And, it is a stroll. He's confident and deadly; you can tell by the way he holds himself. A red and black bandana wraps around his brow without hiding his shaved head. Even this far away, I notice his eyes. They're shards of blue that stand out from the sweat and grime on his face. His chest is bare, with defined muscles that slide beneath the skin as he strides a few steps closer. Dirty sweat trails down his chest in rivulets. The tattoos stand out on his tanned skin. Prison tats from the color. I lift my eyes to his without dissecting the artwork. I've seen few men as stunning as he is. A tingle glides across my nipples and lower to settle between my thighs.

This is what Lorene was talking about and I know who I'm staring at.

My rage from the last hour turns to a low simmer. It's difficult to disregard the sexual signals thrumming through my body. He's tall and younger than most of the other men out here. God decided to play a joke on every red-blooded, dark-skinned woman when he gave this man breath. He should be modeling and not associating with trash. Who am I kidding? He's trash and just because he's attractive doesn't mean he has a brain.

He isn't smiling, but it doesn't take away from his gorgeous face. He has high cheekbones and a square jaw with a few days' stubble. I want to hold his gaze, but I can't stop myself from taking another swipe of his body. I need a bottle of wine and an hour to run my tongue over the crazy ridges on the sides of his abs that lead straight down into mega-man territory.

Am I drooling? I've seen men look at me in a similar fashion. Most I ignore. Every so often, I take one for a ride and fuck his brains out. Nope, won't happen this time; this one belonged to my father. He's a killer just like Frank was. I'll be joining that club soon enough, and, for the craziest reason… I smile.

He smiles back having no clue that I want him to die. The smile is full and sensuous with a dimple on one side of his mouth. My pulse quickens with the need to bite his lower lip and sink my fingernails into his flesh.

*Fuck, stop,* I implore myself silently.

He knows the effect he's having on me because his smile widens. "I'm Dagger. May I help you?" His name on his lips brings me out of the spell he's wrapped around me.

The world goes still. My entire life spirals to this moment—my mother, foster parents, social workers who never cared, and the tears of a scared child with no one to fight for her. Frank…Fox, whatever the fucking name he goes by, my father—is the man who destroyed my mother and killed her unborn children.

The gun is in my hand without a thought. Darkness invades my vision. It all happens so quickly. I aim dead center for his chest. Someone yells, "Gun," beside me. Pull the trigger, I tell myself. Fucking pull. The barrel moves higher—over his head and the gun goes off at almost the same time someone tackles me.

My head hits something hard. Too hard. The bright sun fades to black.

# 7

*Dax*

**What the fucking hell**?" I yell. I run at the woman, but Coke and Loki beat me to her. They take her down hard and she cracks her head against the motor of an old bike.

She doesn't struggle as Loki forces her hands behind her back. She doesn't move at all. Coke jerks her head up and there's a nice gash at the hairline. Coke has her gun. He gives it over when I place my hand out. It's a small .38 revolver. I release the cylinder and spin it to see that one bullet is missing. What the fuck? I've never seen the bitch. For a second, because of her darker skin, I wonder if she's one of Moon's. I don't see Moon sending a woman to kill me, though. He'd send his right-hand man, Gomez, and chances are good I would never see him coming.

"Is she alive?" I ask Loki. He checks her pulse while blood runs down the side of her face and drips into the dirt.

"She's still breathing," he replies.

I'm trying to process what just happened. She asked for me then pointed the gun directly at me. I should have a bullet hole in my chest. A split-second before she pulled the trigger, she shifted the barrel and the bullet went over my head. Why?

"Get her to the small room." I look over my shoulder. "Curly, pull her car around back and bring me everything she has inside. We need to figure out what the hell is going on. Vampire, put some guys on watch. I want the area monitored around the clock until we know why the fuck she almost killed me."

Loki carries her past the women who are standing in the doorway. I'm sure they heard the gunshot from the kitchen.

"You been tastin' chilies on the side, Prez?" one of the brothers asks.

"Shut the fuck up," I tell him. I'm pissed off. Not for the obvious reason that the bitch almost killed me...it's Saturday, one day after I've taken over my new position as president of the Crows. The first order of business was cleaning up the yard. I received a few grumbles and ignored them. As hokey as it sounds, we need bonding time. The only two exempt from the early morning call were Coke and Vampire. They went out last night and buried Fox and Clutch in the desert. They returned early this morning and slept in, not joining us until noon. Things were running smoothly and our sense of camaraderie was growing.

And now fucking this.

The temperature is over a hundred degrees and I promised the guys enough beer to put them under the table if they gave me a full day. Red picked us up a large sub sandwiches for lunch along with the promised beer. The bar at the club has always been a *stock your own* and don't fucking touch another's stash. That's in the wind, and I plan to keep the bar full from here on out. Alcohol isn't any better than drugs but it's legal. I'm prepping for police fallback with the change in leadership. I don't trust Oho and his pal or Pauline as far as I can throw them.

I remove my bandana and wipe my face. I need a shower and one of those beers. But more than that, I need to know who she is and why she fucking aimed a gun at me. I walk over, turn on the hose, and let the water run over my head and chest. I don't bother wiping it off. I'm almost dry before I enter the clubhouse. That's the Arizona heat for you.

Inside isn't much cooler. Fans are going and the evap is running full blast. It only cools things a fraction of what we need to be comfortable. It's something we'll tackle soon. I also need to finish moving myself in. The club needs too much work for me to live at a separate location.

First things first.

I pass Red and tell her to grab me a beer. I walk into the small room while Loki is going through the woman's pockets. She's still out, which isn't a positive sign. Doesn't matter much. Chances are good she won't be leaving this room alive. I hit a woman for the first time yesterday and now I'm thinking about killing one. The thought makes me cringe. Doesn't stop me from knowing it might need to be done. Fuck me.

The biggest question right now is why she pulled the shot. I can't fathom what she was thinking. She checked me out and I read appreciation in her expression. Believe me I was doing the same thing. The woman's hot as fuckin' sin. I examine at her again. Her button shirt is half undone. A black sports bra covers her medium-sized breasts. Early twenties I guess now that I get a better look at her. The blood on her face doesn't hide her refined features or her heritage. She's not just pretty—she's exotically beautiful. Her arms draw my attention away from her face. Even with the shirt covering the upper portions, she carries defined muscle that most women don't have. Takes a lot of work to obtain that kind of physique. Who the fuck is she?

I leave the room and return a minute later with a wet rag. I toss it to Loki because I don't want to touch her. I need to keep this real and the thought of putting my hands on her does something strange to me. Too strange and I'll leave it at that. If she comes to, I won't be adding sexual assault to my criminal jacket. Her fucking body turns my dick into a steel pole. Always thought I went more for the petite ones. Fuck.

She groans when Loki passes the rag over her face.

"I got her things, Prez," Curly says. He has a medium-sized travel bag, a purse, and the paperwork from the car. I take the bag from him and push it against the wall. I loop the purse over my arm. Curly hands me the paperwork and I unfold the white pages.

"It's registered to Sofia Guadalupe Acosta," I say aloud.

The crash of a bottle a few feet from the door to the small room startles me. I look up at Red, who's standing to the side of Curly. Her face is frozen in shock. She dropped the beer and it's spilling all over the floor. Our eyes meet. Fear is unlike Red, but that's exactly what I see. Even yesterday when I planned to remove Pauline's ear, Red wasn't afraid. Squeamish maybe but definitely not afraid.

"Who the fuck is she, Red?"

"I…" she looks behind her and for a moment I think she's going to turn and run. Her eyes come back to mine. She obviously decides it's a foolish decision. "She's Fox's kid."

I'm not sure I hear her right. I met Fox in prison, where he was second in command of the Aryan Brotherhood. I never met a more racially bigoted person in my life. This dark-haired, dark-skinned, Hispanic woman could not possibly be Fox's daughter.

I pass my hand over my stubbled head. "Why the fuck did she just pull a gun on me?"

Red takes a breath, which I'm sure does little to calm her nerves. "She hated her father. I don't know what she was thinking."

"You better come up with something fast." My mind is racing with the possibilities and none of them look good for Red.

She shakes her head, her eyes big as she half leans half falls against the wall.

"Skull," I yell. He comes up behind Red. "Keep Red with you."

Red's voice turns frantic. "I swear I didn't know she would try to kill you. It doesn't make sense. I thought she would be cheering after I called her earlier and told her about her father."

I grab Red's throat, my fingers cutting off her supply of oxygen. "You told someone outside the club that Fox is dead," I say in disbelief. "That's a fucking death sentence, Red. I should get it over with right now."

Her fingernails dig into my wrist as her face turns red and then purple. I finally release her and push her back against Skull as she coughs and gasps for air. "Get her out of my sight." Fuck me. Fuck women. What the hell am I supposed to do with this information? The better question is how the fuck do I keep Red and this woman alive? Not all the brothers are as passive as me when it comes to the treatment of women. Red betrayed us and this woman almost killed me. They'll be lucky if the men don't string them up and have an old-fashioned lynching.

Another moan comes from inside the room. "Bring a cot in here. We have two fold-ups in the storage room," I tell Curly. When he walks off, I address Loki. "Grab the first aid kit and I'll stay with her." The woman is now sitting up. Loki is squatting beside her giving assistance. Her face is buried in her hands. Loki moves away and I take his place. He hustles from the room.

"I don't know what the fuck you think you were doing, but you're in a whole lot of hurt, lady, and it has nothing to do with the gash on your head."

Her laugh is a cross between a squeak and a groan if that's possible. "Maybe the hit to my head will kill me," she says without looking up.

"Would make things simpler on me," I say honestly.

"Go ahead, but make it quick." Her hands move away and her head tilts back. She squints up at me blinking against the bright light from the uncovered single lightbulb in the ceiling. Her large brown eyes capture me.

This is insane. She's so fucking gorgeous that it's hard to pull my eyes away. I should kill her now and put my dick out of its misery. Fuck me but the last thing I want is to add her death to all the other fucked up shit I've done. The problem—she knows her father's dead. I can't trust her to stay quiet. "That would be the easiest for both of us," I say. I shift a little closer. She smells good. I inhale the scent into my lungs while trying to keep it from scrambling my brains even further. I slide a few wisps of hair away from her face and say, "You're lucky I don't like easy."

# 8

*Sofia*

**I pull back a** little from Dagger's hand against my back trying to put some distance between us. I touch my fingers to my forehead. It hurts, and my fingertips come away sticky with blood. There's a dull throb in my head and the light hurts my eyes.

Dagger watches me like I'm an insect he wants to dissect. His blue eyes are ice cold. The smell of dirt and sweat dripping from this man overpowers the room. There's something wrong with my female wiring because I want to rub my nose along his skin. I want to lick the salt crystals that outline the trails of sweat. And I still want to bite that damn bottom lip of his.

He's a Desert Crow. A skinhead. One of the reasons my mother feared for her life. What the hell is wrong with me? I've dreamed of killing my father for so long. This man took it away.

I'm rocked by the knowledge that I have nothing to live for. My world is upside-down and hurt swells inside my soul. The last person I want to see me come apart is this man. I blink back tears. Fucking tears. I hate them. Instead, I concentrate on the dirty, ugly walls with patched holes. The room is completely bare, the floor is rough wood, and the ceiling is stained yellow. Seeing the stains helps me control my emotions because if the yellow isn't water, one or more guys took aim at the ceiling and pissed straight up.

They will kill me—the only question is when. Lorene can't help me; she has her own trouble. I force myself to face Dagger. His eyes have small crinkles at the sides now. If I didn't know better, I'd think they hold compassion. I'm startled away from those deep blue depths when there's a noise at the door. I turn my head and watch the man I saw when I first regained consciousness enter the room with a first aid kit. Behind him, another man enters with a folding cot and a chair. It's a small room, and Dagger and I are sitting dead center on the floor. The two men at the door stay back. I release a small gasp when Dagger lifts and cradles me against his chest. I weigh one forty on a good day. He steps back suddenly and I have no choice but to grab his shoulders. He backs into the corner as the men unburden themselves. Dagger doesn't look at me. He keeps his eyes glued to the two men setting up the cot and chair. I glance down and see a brace on his left wrist that I hadn't noticed before. I notice bruises and swelling beneath the dirt on his arm.

"Curly," Dagger barks, and I grip him a little tighter in surprise, "bring another cloth and some warm soapy water along with a beer and a bottle of water."

Curly gives me the stink eyes and makes sure I know he's not happy. He makes a low grumble deep in his throat before leaving the room.

"Anything else, Prez?" the other man asks.

"Tell the ladies we need to eat in the next hour." This man doesn't hesitate or look at me before walking out.

Dagger stares at the door for a moment before releasing my legs as if it's an afterthought. I slide down his body and his slick warm skin hits my sensitive flesh. I realize my shirt is unbuttoned. Hell, my nipples turn to pinpoints beneath the tight material of my sports bra. As soon as my feet hit the floor I try to pull away. Unexpected dizziness swamps me. The dull throb in my head intensifies and I groan softly. Dagger steers me to the cot and I gratefully sit down. I cover my eyes and take deep breaths.

I glance up when Curly enters again with a large bowl and dry cloth. He sets them beside me on the cot and continues giving me *the look*. Does he think he's scaring me? If he doesn't stop with the attitude, I'll knock the scraggly hair off his chin.

My anger is back and simmering, just waiting to unleash.

"Thanks, Curly, I got this." Dagger's voice thrums inside my head. Not in a good way. The ache from a few minutes ago turns to a steady pound.

"Humph," Curly replies before he walks out. Dagger strolls over and closes the door behind him.

Now we're alone in the room again and I don't know where to look. I reach for the cloth to place it in the water. Dagger steps up and wedges one jeans-clad knee between mine. I'm surprised enough to look up. His eyes burn into me. It's the strangest thing, really. My body is so aware of him. My breasts tingle, my hands sizzle with the need to reach out and touch him.

I don't know what he reads on my face but his eyes have gone cold again and his voice is even more intimidating. "Put down the cloth."

I'm no good at following orders, never have been, especially those given by men. I have no idea why the cloth slips from my fingers and lands in the bowl. Dagger leans in and picks it up. His chest is inches from my eyes and his tats fill my vision. The ink appears prison-grade, but the artwork is intricate. A Grim Reaper stands over a crying woman holding a swaddled baby. The design weaves into swirls of flowers with branches that turn to thorns as they flow further out across his chest. It's devastatingly beautiful in a dark, haunting way.

"While I clean your face, you'll answer my questions."

I have my own question and it centers on the tattoo. I shake off the empathy the artwork invokes. The tone of Dagger's voice helps. Harsh and demanding has never worked in anyone's favor when dealing with me. Mr. Boss Man is about to find out that pushing my buttons is not going to work. "And if I don't?" It would have sounded tough if I hadn't winced when the cloth touched the edge of the cut on my forehead.

The cloth goes still. "You have no idea the fucking trouble you're in, princess." He leans in closer so his hot breath hits my cheek. "I don't think you really want to find out."

My hands form fists and it takes everything I have not to leap up and deck him. "I'm sure I won't be the first Latina you've killed, nor will I be the last," I say instead, keeping my voice as steady as possible.

The fingers of his injured wrist grasp my chin and he raises my head higher. "You actually think the worst thing I could do is kill you?"

I glare at him and allow my rage to build. It's a warm rock inside my chest and it's growing hotter. "I never thought you'd be into brown skin," I taunt, his gut-wrenching tattoo completely forgotten.

He laughs. It's not a happy sound and it sends chills down my spine. "To me and my men," he puts the emphasis on *men* and his smile disappears, "all pussy is pink where it counts."

Heat rises in my cheeks. Fucking asshole.

It doesn't escape me that he's willing to pass me around his men either. And he's not finished handing out threats. "Dying is the easy part, it's what leads up to it that you need to fear."

Fear is not something I'm accustomed to and I don't plan to give into it now. Good looks aside, Dagger is just like my father. If I weren't so dehydrated, I'd spit on him.

He tips my chin up until my neck is all the way back, placing my head at an uncomfortable angle. My hands go to his. They're like iron. "First question: Was Fox your father?"

I was groggy, but I clearly heard Lorene, who they call Red, spill the beans. This small detail is of no consequence. How much do I want to share before they kill me? Dagger eases his grip and I tell him the truth. "Frank Tison, who you call Fox, *was* my father." It's actually nice to emphasize the past tense even though I didn't cause his demise.

"How old are you?"

I have no idea why he cares. "Twenty-six."

"I figured younger."

Most people do.

He goes back to cleaning my face. The water feels good in the hot room. I wiggle a bit because his knee is pressed between my thighs intimately. Too intimately for my tastes.

"See, that wasn't so hard, was it?" He doesn't let me answer. "Who knows you're here?"

Do I want them thinking they're fucked if they kill me? I think so. No good reason for me to answer this question. I remain quiet and Dagger continues cleaning my face. When he's finished, he opens the first aid kit and pulls out a butterfly bandage and some ointment. He's being deceptively quiet and it worries me more than if he threatened me again. He's methodical in his doctoring skills, I'll give him that. When finished, he rests everything on the cot and calmly buttons my shirt, which I had forgotten about. His fingers skim across my hot skin and I inhale sharply. This doesn't go unnoticed. He looks at me with a calculated stare. I break eye contact and glance over his shoulder at the closed door.

He finally steps back, removing the pressure from between my legs. I immediately want it back. My pussy throbs to the same beat as my aching head. God, what I would give to hump his leg right now. This man has me caught somewhere between anger and lust. I have a healthy sex drive, always have. I'm usually discerning, though. Skinhead assholes have never been on my radar. Just the opposite. Yesterday the last person on earth I would want to fuck is the man before me.

He's watching me closely. "You sure you don't want to answer the question?" His eyes darken from steamy pools of light blue to hard, murky ocean waters when I refuse to speak.

He lifts his hand and for a moment I think he's going to hit me. I don't flinch. I've taken beatings—I can handle what he dishes out. Pain and I are old friends.

I'm shocked when his fingers run through my hair. Pins and needles feather over my scalp and he's not even touching me. I want to lean into his fingers like a cat and purr. We're caught in some kind of hot, fucking sexual daze. My gaze lowers. I can see his cock straining against his jeans, proving we're both aware of the invisible sexual burn between us. My gaze slides up over his ripped abs and bulging pecs. The pulse at his throat beats fast. I glance higher and our eyes lock. I want to eat him, lick him, devour him. His eyes tell me he wants the same.

The spell breaks when one of his men enters the room. Dagger takes a bottle of water from the guy, uncaps it, and hands it to me. I'm too thirsty not to gulp down as much as possible. I watch Dagger while drinking it. He grabs his beer, twists off the top, and takes a healthy pull before giving it back to the other man. "Find Skull and have him bring Red in here. I'll need some rope."

I almost spit out the water in my mouth. How stupid can I be? For a moment I thought there was something more between us than an unspoken answer to his question. My anger flashes back to atomic levels. Anger keeps me grounded, and no matter the ache in my pussy, I need to keep the fury at the forefront.

So, what the fuck do I do now? I knew when I began this trip that my death would most likely be the outcome. I never planned for Lorene to suffer punishment for my sins.

# 9

*Dax*

**The kickass look in** her eyes makes my dick hard. The burn of desire is gone and now she burns with hatred. And all that hatred centers on me. I know exactly where she gets her temper. Fox was like that too. Hot and cold. Warm never worked into the equation for him. I guess I'm convinced she's who she says she is. Why the hell would a Hispanic woman show up at this club? There's not exactly a welcome mat out front for anyone with dark skin. Claiming to be his daughter is too crazy not to be true.

Red enters the room with Skull following closely behind. She doesn't show fear, which could work out very badly for her. I stand and move the chair several feet away from Sofia. I look at Red and gesture for her to sit. I roughly jerk her hands behind the back of the chair. She doesn't resist. Skull moves in and takes over with the rope, securing her tightly. His face is grim.

"You need to make noise," I whisper in Red's ear. I hope she understands what I'm telling her. This won't be pretty, but she's a stubborn bitch and I know she can handle what's about to happen without making the sounds required for it to work in her favor.

I glance over my shoulder. Sofia's eyes are dark pinpoints of loathing, her jaw compressed tightly. She regrets firing over my head and it's written plainly in her expression. Red needs to suffer the consequences of her betrayal and this is the only way it might work without her buried six feet under.

Protecting a child is one thing. It's quite another to protect a woman who holds secrets to the club and betrays us. In Sofia's case, she knows entirely too much. The question is… how far am I willing to go? Shooting them both would be easier than torture in my book.

"Skull, hold our Latina visitor."

Skull moves fast, but Sofia is off the cot before he reaches her. She circles around me eyeing the door. She'd need to go through both of us to get out of the room. Her expression changes, and running away is no longer part of her plan. She attacks me with the force of a tiger. Not with claws, though. Fists and feet are her weapons and she's fucking quick. She circles and keeps me between her and Skull. Where the fuck did she learn to fight this way? I take a strike to my jaw, which whips my head to the side and rattles my teeth.

"Back off," I tell Skull.

If she wants to play, I'll oblige.

The room is small, but that doesn't detour her assault. She leaps over Red. Fucking almost flies. Her legs sweep out as soon as she's on the other side of the chair, and I teeter and almost fall on Red. Skull's back is flat against the wall by the cot. I only looked at him for a split second, when Sofia's foot connects with my jaw in the exact place she hit me before.

Bitch!

I take a step back.

"Come on, pretty boy," she says through gritted teeth. "Afraid the Latina will kick your ass?"

She's fucking amazing. No fear, just enough fucking hatred to burn the clubhouse to the ground. I don't see a chance of putting an end to this without hurting her. Hurting me doesn't seem to be a problem for her, so fuck it.

I feign to the right, left, and right again. Prison taught me a lot. There are plenty of guys inside with the ability to fight. Sofia's expecting the first and second move. Not the third. She moves to my left side as I do a half turn and plow my forearm into her stomach.

The air woofs from her lungs and I grab her and lift her from the floor. We're facing each other and I'm ready for a head butt. Instead, she lands a solid kick in my thigh with her shoe. Her movement causes pain in my broken wrist too. Her hands come up and she grabs my ears almost ripping the fuckers off. I grunt. Damn that hurt. Her nails rake the skin of my upper arm. She's fucking strong and almost impossible to control. She moans when I tighten my hold with one arm and grab a handful of her hair with the other. This time her fingernails dig into the side of my face.

"You fucking little bitch," I hiss. "Skull, grab another chair and we'll tie her to it too." I huff out with exertion. I drag her to the cot and take her down. More scrambling ensues as I roll her to her belly so I'm lying half on her with her face pushed into the cot's thin mattress. I hold her like this while waiting for Skull to come back with a chair. I don't give a flying fuck if she can breathe or not. My ears burn like a motherfucker. She bucks beneath me and my dick rises to attention again. What is it about this hellion that turns me the fuck on?

I like petite. She's not even close. I like soft. Sofia is rock hard, especially with her muscles straining beneath me. She's nothing like Savannah. At least my wife had a brain in her head. Sofia is more wrath than calculation. Savannah used her woman's gifts to gain just about anything she wanted. It worked every time. This woman spits vinegar with a world-class right hook to back it up.

I'm aware of Red watching us with interest. I know she's also aware of my hard dick. If she smirks, I'll fucking carry her to the front room and toss her through the window. It will accomplish what needs doing with some added blood and pain involved.

When Skull brings the chair in, I jerk Sofia up by her hair. She gasps for air and continues fighting. It takes both of us to tie her down. Her hair is a wild tumble around her face and even that turns me on. I'm a fucking freak when it comes to this woman. I need to get out of here and jack off.

Fuck it.

"Give me a minute," I tell Skull when I'm sure she's secured. I charge from the room and head across the hall to Fox's old room. Last night, I tossed out everything that belonged to him. One of the whores washed the filthy, threadbare sheets for me so I could at least sleep in the bed. I head into the bathroom and shove my pants to my knees. I groan loudly when my fingers wrap around my cock. I don't bother with slow and controlled. I jack off to the picture in my mind of Sofia tied to that damn chair and give another groan when, two minutes later, I come hard enough to hit the lid of the toilet seat. I rest my palm against the back wall with my head down doing my best to control my breathing as the initial waves pass.

Even her name sounds good on my lips when I whisper it. "Sofia," I say again and fuck me if my dick doesn't jump. This woman will be the death of me.

I finally pull my pants up and secure my belt. When I turn away from the grimy toilet, I slam my fist through the wall by the door. I need the pain. One fucking day as president and this is what I get. A hand job, a pissed off Latina woman, and an ex-junky who needs a lesson in keeping her fucking trap shut.

I leave the bedroom and find Skull standing in the hallway with his arms crossed. He glares at me and shakes his head. Yeah, he knows exactly what I was doing. Fuck, I'm a sicko. I brush past him and enter the small room. Sofia's fury greets me. I stop a foot away from her and move the wild hair covering her face behind her ears so she can clearly see what's about to happen. Her glare burns brighter, and I'm surprised I don't combust on the spot. Shit, my dick is already hardening again.

I drop my hand to the sheath at my waist, unsnap the top strap, and slide the knife free. Her eyes follow the knife as I walk over to the other chair. Red surprises me when she makes a high-pitched keening noise. Either she's playing my game or she's actually afraid.

Here goes every karma point I gained by saving Kiley.

I grab a fistful of Red's hair. "You betrayed our club and placed every member in danger." Red tries to look at Sofia, but I force her attention back to me. "It's just me and you, Red. Nothing she can do. Every man in this club needs to hear you scream."

Red actually rolls her eyes. "Just fucking do it."

Keeping my fingers gripped in her hair, I move slightly behind her and slide the knife up to her cheek without breaking skin. I need this to bleed and it needs to scar. If the brothers think I go too light, it's all for nothing.

"You fucking bastard," Sofia growls.

I offer a tight smile. "Who else knows about Fox's death and where you are?"

Sofia presses her lips together and turns her head away. Red remains quiet when I add more pressure with the knife. "Skull, see that she watches this." I nod to Sofia.

Skull has an old lady he cares about. The two of them had planned to rescue Kiley, but I stepped in before they put their plan into action. Now he's my VP. Whether he likes it or not, this is part of his job. I hope he understands this is the only way to save Red. Fox would slit Red's and Sofia's throats without a second thought.

Skull moves behind Sofia and grabs her head between his large hands forcing her to look in my direction. I left the door open so the brothers would know what's happening in here. I want them to hear Red scream. "Make it good, Red, and the second cut won't be as bad," I say as I make a precise, three-inch cut down her face. Her scream startles me even though I asked for it. Perfect. I sheath the knife and walk over to Sofia. In one strong tear, I rip her shirt open, take my knife out, and cut it all the way off. She still refuses to speak and her eyes continue shooting fire. The rapid rise and fall of her breasts is the only other sign that this is having an effect on her.

I carry the shredded material over to Red and press a section of the shirt to the wound. She hisses when I do it. The cut will require stitches and it's exactly what I intended. She's breathing hard. I give her a moment to calm down. There's a steely light in her hazel eyes when she looks up at me. I palm the uncut side of her face and force her head in Sofia's direction.

"Who knows you're here?" I ask again.

Sofia remains stoically quiet.

I force myself to smile as I trail the dull side of the knife ever so slowly down Red's throat until I'm at the top of her breast. She's wearing a low-cut black tank top. I turn the knife. This cut isn't as deep, but Red lets out a bloodcurdling scream all the same. I'm at my limit for this and hope like hell it doesn't show in my expression.

Sofia's face remains equal parts fury and hatred. "No one knows I'm here, you fucking bastard," she sneers. "You want to cut someone up, try me. I'll scream all you fucking want. Does that get your dick harder, asshole?"

Relief slides through me. Hopefully what I've done will save Red's life. The cut on her breast won't require stitches. Red knows she's getting off easy even if Sofia doesn't realize it.

"Why should I believe you?" I ask as I run the dull side of the blade back up to Red's unmarred cheek.

Sofia's angry expression stays in place. "Because I don't have a fucking person in this entire goddamned world who gives a fuck about me. No one. I'm a byproduct of a drugged out mother and the asshole you killed." The desolation rolls off her in waves. I believe her. I glance at Skull and he nods.

My attention returns to Red. "Some of the brothers will still want you dead. Lay low for a few days. Skull and I will have your back. I'm doing everything I can to save your ass, Red, so in the future, keep your fucking mouth closed about club business. Do you feel me?"

"Yes," she replies quietly.

"Your punishment's over as long as the princess cooperates." At a nod to Skull, he helps me untie Red from her chair.

I address Skull next. "Red stays at the clubhouse until we know things are settled. Only put men on her that you trust. Take the first aid kit with you and lead her past the men before cleaning her up. They need to see the blood."

Skull gestures with his chin to Sofia. "What about her?" he asks.

"We'll have church after we eat and the new board will decide." I run my hand across my stubbled chin. I need to shave, I need to eat, and most of all I need a strong drink.

Skull keeps his voice low when he says, "You may get away with this for Red, but they'll want the woman dead."

"I'll handle them," I say with more conviction than I feel.

I shift my gaze to Sofia. Her hands clench in and out. My fucking cock likes her attitude. There's no way she would have survived killing Fox. It's just like me rescuing Kiley and challenging him. A suicide mission. We're both fucking crazy and because I survived Fox, maybe she can survive a vote.

A month from now, after the club dust settles, this would be far easier to pull off. Right now is not the time for her little plot. Doesn't mean I don't respect her. I just want to know why she aimed that gun at me. Won't matter to the men that she didn't shoot me. She's a liability we can't afford.

# 10

*Sofia*

**The anger burns like** a red hot swell of molten lava.

I thought I could do it. If Dagger cut me, I would have embraced the pain like I do when I fight. Putting the pain on someone else is different. I couldn't watch Lorene…Red…suffer and now Dagger knows my weakness.

The bottom line is I'll be dead tomorrow. If I'd had a gun a few minutes ago, I'd have shot Dagger and Skull both and then taken out as many Desert Crows as I could before they took me down. That's what the anger does. When it takes over and rage fills me, I need blood.

Anger management issues is what the high school counselor said in one of the many meetings my mother and I had with school officials. All I know is that something happens and I have little control when it does. I actually envied the emo girls who cut themselves back then. It relieved whatever demons they carried. Funny, I'd have cut them if they asked.  The only relief I get is from fighting and doing damage to my opponent or getting my ass kicked. Seeing Dagger cut Red didn't bother me. Seeing her helpless and hearing her scream did.

I'm not sure if I believe what Dagger said about saving Red from his men. She knew the consequences if anyone ever found out about her helping me and my mother. This is the price she pays. I owe her, though. It's a debt I'm willing to pay with my own life. If Dagger is right and a few cuts will do the trick, my debt will go to him. That sucks balls. He's a fucking skinhead and I can't ever forget it. Doesn't matter that he's sexy as hell. I noticed the bulge in his pants when he tied me up. I also know why he left the room, the dirty fuck. I'd have liked to watch him jack off. I look up from the floor and see that he's still staring at me. I wonder if he has any idea what I'm thinking.

He closes the door behind Skull and then walks over and turns my chair toward the cot. He sits down and I notice another bulge in his pants. He doesn't appear to give a fuck that I know he's turned on. He reaches down and adjusts his cock and then goes back to staring at me.

"What?" I finally snap as my irritation rises.

"You're not in control, Sofia, and I'm guessing that's the hardest part for you."

"What the fuck are you talking about?"

Even his chuckled huff irritates me. "You're actually easy to figure out. Your shirt's torn off, you have a nice sized bump on your head, and you're knocking on death's door. Doesn't matter; you sit there like a princess on her throne. That's control and you reek of it. So my guess is losing your power makes you angry. Anger makes you want to kill someone." He leans in and places his elbows on his spread knees. "Is that why you wanted to kill me? I…" he moves even closer, "took away your chance to kill your father."

He can't fucking read me this easily. I don't think about what I do next. I spit full in his face. I expect him to slap me. He rears back. Anger flashes in his eyes before his expression changes. Very slowly he smiles. Not a small one or with lips tight—an all-out *happy* smile. He wipes the spit from his cheek and brings the tip of his finger to his lips.

"You even taste good," he says with the smile still in place.

God, fuck, now I'm the one turned on. "You're fucking crazy," I reply.

His eyes crinkle when his smile widens further. "Why did you want to kill me, princess?"

All I want to do right now is fuck his brains out. "Untie me and I'll tell you," I say in a soft whisper.

He enjoys this game. "I don't think so. You see," he looks at my cleavage before lifting his gaze, "I'm in charge and you'll play by my rules. I'd really hate to bring Red back in here. I think she's suffered enough, don't you?"

I try to fight the spell he's casting over me with his soft, coaxing voice. If my hands were untied, I would place my fingers inside my pants and get myself off. It would serve him right. I squeeze my legs together and try to relieve the heat that's growing hotter.

He's right, though. I hate not having control. It brings back memories of going from one foster home to another. I need to be thinking about escaping this hellhole. I'm not above using my body to do it. I'll try sympathy first, though.

I unclench my teeth and lower my voice. "From as far back as I can remember, I've hated Frank Tison and wanted him dead." Dagger's smile disappears. "He got my mother addicted to drugs and made her life a living hell. Even after she escaped, she lived in fear that he would find us. She never managed to beat the habit he started." I look down at my lap and take a slow steady breath so I'm able to continue in the same soft tone. When I look up, the compassion is back in Dagger's expression and I know I'm getting somewhere. "I've had one goal for as long as I can remember. Kill Frank Tison." I bite out the last sentence.

"So why me?" Dagger whispers.

I shrug even though I give him an answer. "So simple really… you took my revenge from me—destroyed everything I've lived for. So…" I let it hang before continuing, "what's one less racist in this world? I don't think anyone would cry if you died."

He leans back suddenly and his expression goes blank. The words hit him hard and I wonder about the secrets he keeps buried. He stands and walks over to the wall and grabs my purse. He rummages inside and removes my phone. He looks at the call history. One number, three phone calls. Doesn't surprise me that he checks.

I lick my dry lips. Dagger misses nothing. He grabs the water bottle from the floor and tips it to my lips so I can drink. "Thank you," I mutter.

He gathers up the items in the room—my purse, phone, travel bag, and bloody shirt. He doesn't look at me when he walks to the door. "Some major shit will go down because of you and Red. I'll have one of the men check on you." Without untying me, he closes the door. I hear the sound of a key and know I'm locked in.

What the hell did I expect? They'll kill me soon. I don't feel sorry for myself. Relief maybe. I brought this shit down and now it's time to pay up. I close my eyes and try to relax. Maybe this would be a good time to start meditating. Years ago, a therapist provided by social services recommended it. I laughed at her while I screamed inside.

My life has been one long, silent, scream.

# 11

*Dax*

**I shouldn't fucking care.** She's no one to me, but I still replay everything she said. What kind of hell did she live through? Twenty plus years is a long time to plan vengeance and keep the torch burning. How can I not respect that? If I hadn't killed the man who killed Savannah and my child, I would still want vengeance.

I walk into the front room, where the men are waiting. The only woman in the room is Red. She wisely keeps her eyes down. The men congregate in groups talking quietly. I march behind the bar and grab a beer out of the fridge, untwist the top, and take a healthy swig. I need another minute to gather my thoughts.

I rest the beer on top of the long, marred counter before looking over the room. "We eat and then the officers will meet at the table to discuss what we do with the woman."

Bear is one of the only men standing. "You need to hold church for that? She should already be dead," he grumbles.

I give him my full attention. "I'm not Fox. I don't kill women without a very good fucking reason."

He's not intimated, which is what worries me about not acting decisively on this.

"She pointed a gun at you. She knows you killed Fox. Red says she's his fucking kid even if it's hard to believe. I say get it over with and let's move on," Bear says.

He's a cold bastard and I wonder why he's still here. Skull put in a good word for him or I'd be knocking him on his ass right now. He's saying what several of them feel, I'm sure of it. I hold my temper and thankfully it's AJ who settles things down.

He stands and faces off with Bear. "We're a club. The officers vote for what's best for the club. Our prez isn't dictating, he's acting responsibly. Have you fucking forgotten that Fox was a tyrant and did whatever the fuck he wanted whenever the fuck he wanted to?" He glances at me. "I agree with you. We hold church after eating because right now, I'm fucking starving."

"Here, here," Skull shouts and tips back his beer. Bear mutters under his breath but doesn't say anything more. He grabs a chair and falls into it. The old chair squeaks under his weight. Bear's around my age, packs close to the same muscle as I do, and carries a huge chip on his shoulder much like the woman in the small room. I heard he did time for beating a man to death. Given my own past, I can hardly judge. I'm keeping my eyes on him, though.

It twists my guts that I already know the way this vote will go. I'll be the one to fucking pull the trigger too. I won't leave this to Skull or Vampire. I'm now wearing the president's patch and that patch comes with a price. I remove another beer and drink it down as quickly as the first.

The women made enough chili to feed a village. It's halfway decent—burns fire through my intestines and has enough salt to raise my blood pressure significantly. Arizona red bottom chili at its best. Hell, I'm starving and willing to eat almost anything. At least this is slightly better than the TV dinners I've been living off. The clubhouse has never been known for its fine cuisine. Chips or bags of peanuts are the usual fare. It's something else I plan to change. We need to be a family and that means we spend time together. Fox had monthly "bring your own everything" barbeques and that was the only "family time" as far as including old ladies was concerned. Besides the barbeques, Fox never wanted girlfriends or old ladies at the club or even on the property. Fridays and Saturdays were brother party nights when the whores earned their drugs.

One of my priorities is making room on the property for the single men. If the tied brothers want to move onto the property, they're welcome to. The more the merrier. We need to make sure everyone is financially sound and doesn't do something stupid that lands them back behind bars. I've taken over Fox's room and that leaves two other available rooms plus the small room. We'll save that one for unexpected visitors. If we didn't need every penny to get a convenience store started, I'd tear down the clubhouse and build from the ground up. Aluminum siding on the outside and painting on the inside will need to do for the next year.

Years ago, this land was a motorhome park. It still has the hookups but they're so old we need the electricity cleared by the county. Once that happens, we can build our own small city. It would solve so many problems.

There's very little talk while we eat. The earlier camaraderie from working together outside is gone. The only bright spot is having the front yard of the clubhouse cleared. We'll tackle the back yard in the next few weeks.

I hold back a groan at all the shit I need to do.

The chili sets heavy in my stomach when I stand and walk to the meeting room. I glance over my shoulder and the other board members rise and follow.

The room is about ten by fifteen with enough space for a large table and chairs. There are folding chairs stacked against the far wall and that's it. The room has a ceiling fan and one small boarded window, so the fan mostly circulates the heat.

I walk to the head of the table and pull out *the* chair. Even though I fucking hated Fox, it's strange to take his seat. I wasn't part of the inner sanctum and rarely entered this room. I knew the rule, though—no one sat here but Fox. I pick up the old wooden gavel lying on the table and run my hand over the smooth handle. I glance up and see the brothers watching me.

"Fucking weird," I say aloud. A second later, I rap the wood sharply on the table.

Church is in session.

Skull, Vampire, Johns, and AJ wait for me to begin. "Honestly, this isn't what I expected on day two as president." I scratch my chin and continue. "We have a tough decision and nothing about it makes me fucking happy."

Skull grunts and AJ starts to speak but then decides against it.

I look at him and then share my gaze with each of them. "At this table we speak our minds. I'm not Fox, and if this club goes down, it will be on us as a group. It doesn't matter if we agree or disagree in this room. Majority vote carries and when we leave this room, we back it up." I direct my gaze to AJ. "Say what the hell you need to say."

He clears his throat before speaking. "Red's a problem too and it seems you're overlooking it. Her fuck up could send us back to prison. We don't know who else knows what went down yesterday. Killin' a woman ain't my thing. That said... both of them are a danger to this club."

My hands are flat on the table and I fight balling them into fists. I knew Red would be a problem. I also know AJ is right in everything he says. "Pauline is a danger to us too and she walked away." I'm hoping this puts things into perspective. "The men who left the club yesterday walked out with all of our secrets. I'm not stupid and I know we haven't seen the last of them."

"What did Red say?" Vampire asks.

I turn to Vamp. "Not much. I didn't really give her a chance to explain before I punished her." I give AJ a quick head bob. "I made it severe enough to leave a lasting memory if she ever decides to share again."

Skull speaks up next. "Fox never gave a fuck about the women. I know they stuck around because of the drugs, but, like us, they have no place to go. They've put up with a lot of our shit. I think we owe them a say. What's strange is that Fox kept Red around instead of kicking her ass to the curb like he eventually did to all the other women who spread their legs for him. I'd like to know more about that connection and give Red a chance to defend her actions."

If I didn't know better, I would think Skull had a background in communication. That was a damn eloquent speech. I glance around the table. "Are we voting on it?"

"I'm a go for Red having her say," AJ says, and the other men nod.

"Bring her in, Skull."

His chair slides back and he leaves the room. A few minutes later, he leads Red in. I can't read her expression. Skull gives her his chair and grabs one from against the wall. Red meets everyone's eyes with a little more belligerence than she should. Fucking woman could use a lesson or two in humility. She's not stupid and must know why she's here.

"Everything, Red. Leave nothing out," I say. Skull stitched her face and I have no doubt it hurt like a bitch. The skin around the bandage is red and puffy. Another smaller bandage covers the top part of her breast. It was little more than a scratch of my knife, but I'm hoping it means something to the men in this room.

Red's long fingernails tap against the table for a moment as if she's considering. I swear I'll strangle her if she keeps this up. "I'll tell you whatever you need to know," she finally says sweetly.

For her sake, I hope she gives us something that will keep her alive. "Start from the beginning," I nudge when she doesn't begin talking immediately.

She rests her palms flat on the table and the infernal clicking stops. She exhales loudly before she begins the story. I'm not feeling the regret for what she did. If *I'm* not, no one the fuck else is either.

"I met Sofia's mother, Carmen, when Fox brought her to the bar where I worked." She stares at the wall over AJ's shoulder before continuing. "Fox and I fucked regular back then. One day, he shows up with this young, beautiful thing on the back of his bike. I'll admit I was pissed off. Carmen was so innocently pure it was enough to gag you. No one understood what the hell she was doing with Fox. He had the hots for her big time. And he wasn't as particular back then when it came to skin color. Perry ran the club and had a Native American old lady. You all know that, years later, Fox killed both of them and changed the club to what it was until yesterday." She takes her eyes from the wall and gives equal attention to everyone at the table. She shakes her head. "Carmen was sweet, vivacious, and incredibly beautiful. You've seen her daughter. The two are very similar. Her English wasn't too good, but she caught on quick. Fox could be quite the ladies' man when he took the time." She makes a disgusted face like it pained her to say that. "I watched him devour her completely. He pressured her into using drugs and verbally dragged her down until the drugs were her only escape. It only took a few months before she was addicted and relied on Fox for everything. Once she craved what he provided, he started beating the shit out of her for every small infraction. He called her his Mexican punching bag and said he liked the way she screamed." Red stops and her eyes turn back to the wall. It's obvious she doesn't like replaying these memories. She clears her throat. "Speaking Spanish was one of his major issues. He almost killed her once for saying, 'gracias'."

Red glances down at her hands, which are now in fists. "I tried to talk her into leaving him but the drugs held her. I could barely keep up with my own drug habit back then, so I kind of understood." Red gives a small laugh and her fingernails start clicking again. "Jesus, I won't deny it. I was glad Fox had someone besides me to beat on." Her fingers stop moving and she stays silent for a moment. All I can hear in the room is the clank of the ceiling fan. "He began sharing her with his friends. That was the hardest part for her. She'd take a beating, but shit, she hated sex with all those men. I walked a street corner down on Van Buren before I met up with Fox, so sleepin' with different guys was no big deal for me. Shame was what really controlled Carmen. She'd beg Fox not to loan her out until he beat the shit out of her, stripped her naked, and let those men gangbang her." Tears roll down Red's face and I hope like hell they affect the men around this table.

"Go on, Red," I encourage softly.

"She was pregnant twice before Sofia." She wipes her eyes with trembling hands. "Fox beat those babies out of her. It's a miracle he didn't kill her. Then she discovered she was pregnant with Sofia. She was a dried up old woman and not even thirty." She looks into AJ's eyes. Wisely, she knows he's the one she needs to convince. "I betrayed Fox and helped her get away. I'd do it again too. I'll pay with my life knowing that I did something good."

Red takes her eyes from AJ and scans the table. "Fox swore he'd find her and kill her. He looked everywhere. Eventually, one of the boys tagged her walking into a grocery store when Sofia was a year old. When Fox didn't arrive at the store in time to confront her, he practically screamed this place down. He staked out the store for two weeks before catching her. He beat her so bad she spent more than a week in the hospital. Thank God she didn't have Sofia with her that day. Fox went down for five years. He served two. By the time he got out, I was off the drugs, but like everyone else here, I had nowhere to go. After Fox did his stint in state, he was more involved in his racial crap too. He got out, took over the club, and made the changes he wanted." She looks at me. "The men back then were too afraid to mention Carmen. Fox would lose his shit if they did. Most of those men fazed out of the club, were killed in the shit Fox had going down, or Fox killed them himself. There's really no one around, now that Clutch is dead, who would remember her. I'm the only whore who goes that far back."

She takes a long breath and lays her cards on the table. "Carmen and I stayed friends and I made sure Fox stayed off her tail.

He vowed to kill her and I have no doubt he would have if given the chance. I owed Carmen and her daughter that peace of mind."

Red reaches up and touches one of the bandages on her cheek. She gazes at me again. "My friendship with Sofia started when she was around eight. Carmen called me off and on through the years. The first time I spoke with Sofia, Carmen was high as a kite and passed out. Sofia picked up the phone. The saddest part… Sofia was only a little girl but her mother sprawled out and unconscious was a way of life. It barely fazed her. I had Sofia write down my number and told her to call me if Carmen wasn't awake the next morning. I didn't hear from either of them for six months. When Carmen called again, she had just received Sofia back from Social Services and swore she was off drugs for good. Sofia was in and out of foster care her entire childhood. Carmen never completely kicked her habit and Sofia found her dead of an overdose about a year ago.

Red's expression changes and anger tightens her lips. "Sofia hated Fox. He killed her unborn siblings, which is something that tortured her. She's told me for years she would kill Fox one day. In this one way, she's just like him. She never forgets." Red zeros in on me again. "Telling her Fox was dead wasn't a betrayal to this club, it was a celebration. Sofia deserved to be free of that man for good. I don't know why she pulled the gun on you. I do know she has a temper and street fights to work out her issues and support herself. Her life has never been easy. I don't care what you do to me, but Sofia is no danger to this club. I told her a week ago about what Fox had planned for Kiley."

Red bites her lip and I can tell she was in the same quandary as many of us. I let her finish her story.

"Sofia was furious and I think that's what finally took her over the edge. Just like you, Dagger. Somehow we all needed to draw a line. Sofia drew hers." Red lifts her hands from the table, sits back, and crosses her arms.

She's done with her story.

AJ looks at me and I give him a nod.

"Why did Fox keep you around?" he questions.

Red keeps her eyes on the table. "When Fox got out of prison for beating Carmen, the club needed whores. I was clean but still had friends who weren't particular about what they did to obtain their drugs." She shrugs. "Fox liked new meat. I guess I just made his life simpler in the long run because I could provide what he wanted."

I have the strangest feeling that Red's lying. I have no idea why, but I'll keep the thought to myself. An idea occurs to me. Curly watches Red closely and everyone knows he has the hots for her. To Fox, the whores were not old ladies, they were nothing more than a hole if you needed to get your rocks off. Curly couldn't claim Red while Fox had the power. Things are different now and it could solve our problem if Curly claimed her.

"If one of the men takes you on as an old lady, will you have a problem with it?"

Red thinks about it for a moment. "I'm sure this is your way to keep me in line. I don't like not having a choice. That said, if it's Curly, I won't complain." Red stands and looks at me. "If you give me the chance, I'll be loyal to you. Never felt that way about Fox."

I nod and she walks out.

The men are silent for several minutes. "That's fucked up shit," Johns says.

I push back a bit in my chair. "We have a chance to turn this club around. Killing women isn't the way we do it."

"If we let that girl leave, the brothers will revolt," AJ says.

He's right. None of us wants to go back to prison and she knows a secret that could jeopardize the entire club. "I think Curly will claim Red. That leaves it to one of us to claim Sofia." Yeah my dick jumps at the thought. Her wanting to be claimed could be a problem, though.

Skull laughs and breaks some of the tension in the room. "You want her, just admit it and make this easier for everyone at this table." He's not stupid. He saw my hard dick before I rubbed one out. She's a load of trouble. Maybe even more trouble than I can handle or want to handle with all the other shit I need to worry about right now. "Yeah," I answer honestly. "I want her." I glance at AJ.

"The brothers won't like it," he says.

"Can they live with it, though?"

He doesn't mince words. "Yesterday this was an all-white club. You've tied us in with Moon's organization and no one knows if that's good or bad. Now you're bringing a Mexican chick in who pointed a gun at you. You tell me."

Fuck-all disaster is what he's saying. "When we walk through those doors, do you have my back?" I ask him.

He nods and I glance at each man in turn.

One by one they look me in the eyes and answer, "Yes."

AJ snickers. "She's a street fighter. You'll have your work cut out for you. I saw the guns on that chick," he says as he laughs. "If she slits your throat in the middle of the night, it's on you. I've got your back with the brothers, Prez. But you better keep her in line. She's stuck with this club for the foreseeable future. It'll take a lot before the brothers trust her."

Relief slowly sinks in. I did it. With a lot of help from Red and now both women have another shot. I have no doubt Red meant what she said about following my lead—Sofia will be an entirely different story. I'll keep them apart for a few days and let things calm down before the brothers see them together.

"Now that the problem with the women is settled, we need to move on to other important shit. We have a shipment arriving Friday night. I don't like it, but it's too late to stop the buy now without starting a war we don't need. If we're lucky, they'll choose not to deal with us when they learn Fox is out of the picture."

We discuss the hazards of the pending buy and discuss how we'll end our relationship with the suppliers. My mind is only half on the discussion.

Sofia is mine for now, she just doesn't know it yet. At least the guys can't see my dick growing hard as I picture the coming explosion.

# 12

*Sofia*

**I'm desperate to pee**. Thirst, hunger, and aching arms don't make the list right now because my bladder comes first at this point. When they kill me, it will serve them right when I piss all over the floor. Fuck, they're probably accustomed to it.

I have no way to keep time. What seems like hours is most likely minutes. I'm really wishing I'd shot Dagger's ass when I had the chance. I've been staring at the same cracks in the walls and connecting them to make pictures. Anything to take my mind off my cramping bladder.

When the door opens, my anger ratchets up ten notches. I turn my head and see a younger man with the prerequisite bald head that's prevalent in this hairless, gorilla society. He pokes his head in, takes one look at me, and backs out.

"Don't you dare close that door. I need to take a piss, you son of a bitch. If you make me wait another minute, I'll piss right here."

He closes the door anyway. I struggle against the rope holding my hands. Fire shoots into my shoulders along with more cramps in my bladder. I'm ready to start screaming my head off, when the door opens and Dagger walks in. He strides over, removes the knife from his hip, and slices through the rope in a matter of seconds. I know it's not the brightest move I've ever made but I come out of the chair swinging. It's not a calculated move. This is desperate rage and wanting to feel my fist slam into Dagger's face. I don't expect him to move as fast as he does. The palm of his hand strikes my chest, hard. Pain ignites and I wouldn't be surprised if he stopped my heart. Fuck, it takes me a moment to collect my thoughts.

"I like you on your back, but I'm not into piss play, so if you really need to go, shut the fuck up, cool your jets, and do what the fuck you're told," he bites out.

I had the chance to kill him and I pulled the fucking gun like an idiot. "Fine," I spit. That word should put the fear of God into him. I scramble off the bed and precede him from the room. He steers me two doors down, reaches in front of me, and opens a door to a bathroom. It's a five by five room with nothing but a filthy toilet and cracked walls. Not even a fucking sink. I enter and try to close the door behind me. Dagger's foot stops me.

"Door stays open," he grits out.

"I'm not pissing with you watching me."

His large hand grasps my arm and I'm halfway back to the room where he's been keeping me before I realize he really doesn't plan to allow me to pee.

"Fine. Stand and watch. If that's how you get your jollies, who am I to stop you?" I hope to God he can't hear the desperation in my voice.

He spins me around and shoves me back toward the bathroom. I waste no time pulling down my jeans and squatting on the toilet. As bad as I need to go, the stream takes a minute to start with him watching. This is so damn humiliating. Made worse by the lift of Dagger's brow when I don't pee right away. The relief is so great when my body finally cooperates that it's hard not to groan. I'm sure he'd like that. I look around for toilet paper and find none.

"Seriously, there's no paper?"

Dagger shrugs.

"What the hell would you do if I took a shit?" I stand and pull my jeans and panties up and do my best to disregard the fact that my panties are now wet. If I get my hands on his knife, I'm cutting off his dick and stuffing it down his throat, I promise myself. I walk back into my prison with a wet crotch and unwashed hands.

"If you promise to behave, I'll leave you untied. The last thing you want to do is leave this room and run into the men. I'm in a meeting and need a bit more time. Finish up the bottled water and I'll be back to feed you as soon as my meeting is over." He actually sounds civil for a change.

"Thank you," I say grudgingly and hope he leaves quickly before I lose my fight to contain my temper.

The door closes, the lock snaps in place, and I jump up and kick the cot. My foot is the only thing that hurts after the tantrum. It doesn't help that I couldn't scream when I did it. I'm sane enough to know I don't need to draw attention to myself. Fucking moron, skinhead, asshole. I picture him with his cock in his mouth. It helps to keep me from kicking the cot again.

I drink the water and ignore my growling belly. Do motorcycle gangs feed someone before they kill them? I lie back on the cot and throw my arm over my eyes. I can't look at another crack or I'll go crazier than I already am.

I'm almost asleep when Dagger finally returns. "You hungry?"

I decide that silence is the best policy or I'll get myself in trouble. I also don't want another shot to the chest, so I keep my hands to myself. I roll on the cot, sit up, and place my feet on the floor. He steps back into the hallway and I'm guessing I won't be eating in this room. He doesn't seem concerned that I don't have a shirt covering my sports bra. It's one of my workout bras and along with a skimpy pair of shorts it's all I usually wear. He'll be sadly disappointed if he thinks it'll bother me. I follow him down the hallway to a large room filled with ugly biker dudes. Maybe some women like the bald, shaggy facial hair type but not me. I like my men with a furless crotch and face along with nice hair I can hang onto when they go down on me.

The men who watch me don't appear happy. That fact and that I'm being fed could mean I have time before they pull the plug. I see a few of the guys zero in on my tits. I straighten my back so they get a good look. Dagger notices and shakes his head like he can't believe I'd use my scantily covered breasts to postpone the amount of time I keep breathing. He doesn't know me well. He pulls a chair out at one of the tables and there's a bowl in front of it. It looks like chili. I sit down, pick up the spoon poking from the bowl, and ignore the men. I'm starving.

The first bite has kick. With my heritage it's not hard to eat the spicy chili. It surprises me that the lily-ass gringos can handle it.

"Fucking bullshit is what this is," one of the men shouts. He comes out of his chair and shoves it back so hard, it tumbles across the floor.

I halt the spoon midway to my mouth and watch Dagger jump on the man, taking him down. He quickly has the guy by the throat. *Smooth move,* I'm thinking when Dagger growls, "It was a unanimous decision. You want to walk, you had your chance. If you want a six-foot hole, challenge me."

The man gasps for air. "She fucking tried to kill you or have you forgotten?"

"She pulled the shot and you fucking know it. I'd be dead if she hadn't." Dagger glances my way and I put the spoon in my mouth like I don't have a care in the world.

*Give me another chance with a gun and I won't miss,* I think while doing my best to convey puppy dog eyes.

Dagger climbs off the man and crosses his arms.

The guy stands and dusts off his jeans. "Look, Dagger, I'm fucking sorry. We all want this club to prosper and I was sick of Fox and his bullshit. I have no love for spics, but I couldn't care less where you put your dick." Dagger takes a menacing step toward the guy and the man raises his hands. "No disrespect, I just have no idea what to call her."

This is actually funny. Spic doesn't bother me. Hell, I've been called much worse. Dagger seems to have a problem with it, which surprises me.

"Her name is Sofia," Dagger grinds out.

The guy nods without bothering to look at me. I'm quite aware this isn't over, but I did learn I have a stay of execution. I keep eating the chili and drink from the water bottle that's beside the bowl.

Dagger pulls out the chair beside me, turns it around, and straddles it. He speaks loudly so all the men hear him. "This is your home for now, princess. You'll be earning your keep cleaning and serving. If you have a problem with that, say it now. Any one of these men, including me, will happily give you a plot of brown earth to rest in."

The longer I'm alive, the better chance I have to escape. And I will escape. "I'll take the first offer," I inform him.

"You start immediately. There's a ton of dishes in the kitchen. The whores will be in here entertaining us."

Whores, really? These Neanderthals need a basic class in… fuck… Basic Humanity 101, maybe. My bitch rises to the surface. "I wouldn't think you'd need to pay for it, but I guess there are quite a few women turned off by premature baldness."

His expression conveys exactly how stupid I am. He grabs my hair and pulls me out of the chair, dragging me from the room. I hear the snickers and do my best to hold back my fists. When I explode and plant Dagger's ass on the ground, it needs to be a surprise and one without witnesses so I can escape.

Dagger shouts behind us, "Rufus, you have guard duty until the damned kitchen is clean. Bring her back in here when she's finished so I can tuck her into bed for the night." The chuckles turn to laughter. Dagger throws a door open and pushes me inside. Rufus, the guy who peeked in on me while I was tied to the chair, enters behind me. Dagger leaves without saying another word. I look at Rufus. He's goofy looking in a young Woody Harrelson kind of way. I'm guessing he's in his early twenties. It's hard to tell with his shaved head. Unlike most of the other men, his face is hairless.

I glance around the kitchen. Not only is it ugly, it's piled high with the filthiest mess I've ever seen. I storm over to the sink and almost vomit. The smell is horrendous and the grime peeking through the dishes is growing fungi. It takes three seconds to realize there is no dishwasher. Dammit, this will be a hand job. I smile internally. I'm not exactly a hand job kind of girl.

I open the cabinet beneath the sink and surprise, surprise find dish soap, bleach, and scouring pads. No rubber gloves, though. I look at my nails. They're not in the best shape to begin with. The polish on them has seen better days. "So much for my velvet soft hands," I mutter jokingly.

I empty the sink while ignoring the guy behind me. I'll be damned if I speak to any of these twat heads. A woman's squeal comes from the front room. God, I hope whoever's out there is of age. A hard-rock beat that I would usually shake my ass to fills the kitchen. I'm tempted to do it even with Rufus Woody standing behind me, but I resist.

When the sink is empty, I start scrubbing the porcelain. I'll be damned if I eat off plates that are cleaned in a smelly sink. My arms are burning before I'm satisfied that I won't die of botulism the next time I eat. The bowl of chili I had earlier is now questionable, but hopefully the spices killed off food poisoning.

I start scraping plates, bowls, pans, and utensils into a garbage can I remove from under the sink. There's no damn dish pan, so I have no choice. When I begin the actual washing, I have time to think. I haven't seen Lorene... Red. I don't see them killing her and leaving me alive. I need to talk to her. She's coming with me when I leave.

According to the clock on the old stove, it takes me more than two hours to clean the kitchen. The more time that passes, the rowdier it gets in the other room. I'm exhausted when I dry the last dish. I had to disregard the fact that I put everything into dusty cabinets. Unless I get out soon, I'll have plenty of time to sanitize the entire room.

Rufus is leaning against the door jamb trying to stay awake. I know the feeling. I walk past him and he follows. There's a very short hallway and it takes only a few steps before I'm back in the large front room.

Fuck.

One of the men has his naked ass on the bar and a woman is sucking his dick like there's no tomorrow. Another woman's laugh gains my attention. Her arms are around Dagger. He's at a table playing cards. The woman is standing slightly to the side behind him. Rufus walks around me and gives Dagger a short whistle. Dagger ignores the hands on his shoulders and stands. The woman steps away and looks unhappy when Dagger walks over to me. She's not exactly pretty, though maybe at some point in her life she was. Now she's skin and bones, obviously from a drug habit. I saw it too many times when I was younger. Dagger nods at me and I guess that means follow. He grabs a beer bottle from the top of the bar, ignoring the woman who's still giving head to one of his men, and walks me back to the cell I was in earlier. I continue past it to the bathroom and open the door. I immediately notice a roll of toilet paper on the floor. I'm surprised when Dagger reaches in and closes the door behind me. Wow. He's allowing me to do my business in private.

I leave the bathroom with trepidation. I'm caught between pissed off and horny. What the hell is it about Dagger? I won't kid myself and deny my attraction to him—bald head and all. I think most women would be attracted to him. I enjoy sex and as long as the man doesn't expect lovey-dovey shit afterward; I use it to work off some of my anger issues. It's everything Dagger stands for that makes me feel caged and apprehensive. If only his bald head was more of a turnoff. Every time I see him he seems a little more...

doable. He has rock fucking solid muscle that makes me check beneath my lips in case I'm drooling. He really needs to wear a shirt. In the few steps we have before entering the room, I check out his back tats. I thought biker gangs wore their patches on their backs. Dagger's work is unfinished and I haven't the foggiest idea what it is. Another tat question that will go unanswered because I refuse to ask.

We reach the room they held me in earlier. Do I fight and pretend I don't want this? Who the hell knew there would be a new, gentler skinhead group when I arrived and sex would even be an issue? God, I try not to laugh at that thought. These men are violent, and coming from me that's saying a lot.

I can't make up my mind so try to stall. "Could you at least tell me if Red's okay?" I add a bit of whining to my tone at the end. Guys think of it as a weakness and I need to plan my escape carefully. I can pretend to be weak.

Dagger follows me into the room without answering and shuts the door behind him. He leans back against the wood and tips the bottle of beer to his mouth. His red eyes convey he's had a little too much to drink. He needs a shower, I can smell him from here, and yet he's still fucking sexy. Swagger literally drips from his pores in waves of confidence that I've rarely seen. My pussy goes wet as I look at every defined angle of his chest and abs. It's not a sock in his pants either. A fucking white boy has never affected me this way.

My heart skips a beat when he speaks. "Take your clothes off. Everything," he orders.

My sensitive nipples throb and my inner thighs sizzle with longing to give him the ride of his life. It sucks that my mind rebels. I hate everything he and his club stand for and I shouldn't be attracted to him.

Fuck it. Easy or hard? I'll enjoy hard more, so what the hell? "Sure you can get your dick up, bald man?"

His hand goes to his head and slides over his scalp. "You tell me," he says lazily. "You can't take your eyes off my fucking body or the bulge in my jeans." He takes another swig of beer. "Remove the fucking clothes, Sofia." His hand moves to his waist and the bigger than shit knife he wears. It's a threat and it pisses me off. This is not the way you play this game.

Without changing the tone of his voice he continues. "Take them off or I'll cut the damn things off and you won't be getting new ones anytime soon. You in that bra contraption was a lot of temptation for my men. How long will you last with nothing covering that pussy of yours?"

He just had to go and ruin everything. "Fuck you," I say because I don't like him threatening me with something he won't carry through on. His cock wants this Latina pussy too damn much to give it to his men.

# 13

*Dax*

**I've had more than** I should to drink but even so, I'm not into raping women. Her hot Latina eyes are impossible to miss when she checks me out. She hates me but wants to fuck me too. We're in the same boat, though I'll admit I don't exactly hate her.

I want her clothes because I'm not sleeping in here or with her at all tonight. Her ass would be too much to resist if we were in the same bed. Her bag and purse are already in my room. I'm hoping the lack of clothes will stop her from running. The burs around the clubhouse will help, so her shoes are coming off too. The side benefit is seeing her naked. And I fucking want to see her naked.

There's a lot riding on her willingness to stay here without causing trouble. I'll discuss the options with her in the morning. Her captivity can go easy or hard. She needs to convince the brothers she's not a threat, and if she can do that, I'll get her away from the mess she caused.

Her eyes are hard pinpoints as she stares back at me in defiance and her, "Fuck you," made my dick twitch.

I flip the knife in the air and catch it by the handle. Not bad for as tipsy as I am. I take one step forward and stop when her fingers go to the snap on her jeans. Her eyes breathe fire. I gesture with the point of the knife and she wiggles the tight material down her sexy curves. Flawless light brown skin and long legs make me take a step back and lean against the door again. I won't touch her, but it's so fucking hard. Hell, I want to grab my dick and jack off to the show. Her hips flair with her rounded ass and curve to a small waist. Not that she's exactly small, but fuck is she perfect. She toes off her athletic shoes and the jeans pool on the floor. She kicks them away and stands in front of me in her bra and panties. The underwear is black like her bra. I like it, and so does my dick.

I take another hit of beer and watch the rest of her strip routine. She grabs the band of the bra and raises it up over her breasts, bringing it high on her arms before dropping her hands and allowing the bra to hit the floor. Her breasts jiggle with the movement. The panties go down next, slowly giving me a view of her hairless pussy. Fuck me but I want to bury my face in it. She stands in front of me only wearing short white socks. She doesn't cross her arms or try to hide herself from my gaze.

My breath catches on a sudden flashback of Savannah. It's like being hit by an ax. The two women are nothing alike and still, seeing Sofia's pride, I'm reminded of the only woman I've ever loved.

I step forward, unable to speak, and pick up the items from the floor. She can keep the fucking socks. I need to get out of this room and away from her. I lock the door behind me and march across the hall to the room I've claimed. I need sleep, dammit. And what do I do? I pull her fucking underwear up to my nose and inhale filling my lungs with the smell of her pussy.

I'm a dirty bastard.

I slam my door, toss the clothes on the bed, and shuck my jeans. My body hits the bed and I grab Sofia's panties from her pile of clothes. I bring them back to my nose. Fuck, I want to eat her pussy. I lower the silky cloth to my cock and jack off again.

I wake up with sunlight shining through the window. Panic sets in when I realize Vampire should have woken me hours ago. He had first watch at the end of the hallway last night. I don't bother pulling on my pants as I charge from the room.

He's resting with his back to Sofia's door.

He opens one eye and says, "Quiet all night, Prez."

I put my hand down and help him off the floor. "Thanks for letting me sleep."

"No problem, but if you don't mind I need to catch some shut-eye."

"Go down the hall. The sheets were changed in there yesterday too."

He weaves down the hall and I go back into my room and grab my jeans before heading to Sofia's door. She sits up from the cot as soon as I walk in. "If you want a shower, now's the only chance you'll have today."

She stands up and I wave for her to follow. Morning wood combined with voluptuous curves make my cock stand at full attention. Poor Vampire may never be the same.

I walk back into my bedroom. It has the only private bath and shower in the building. Not that it's much. I close and lock the bedroom door behind us and open the bathroom door. Sofia walks ahead of me. "Get in and get washed up," I tell her. I head to the toilet and spend a moment trying to get my dick under control so I can relieve myself. She's in the shower before I finish. I shuck my jeans and get in the far end.

"What the hell are you doing?" she yells.

Water slides over her gorgeous body and I'm back to rock hard before I speak. "Taking a shower, princess. I need to start my day sooner rather than later. I'll make it quick unless you want to change my mind." I grab my cock and slide my finger up the length adding a bit of pressure at the head.

"Keep that… that thing away from me." She actually points at my dick.

Her outrage is damn funny and I laugh. I also give myself a healthy massage. "Hand me the soap, will you?"

She whips back the shower curtain and all I can grab in time is her hair. "If you don't want to take care of the problem, I will. You aren't getting out until I say so."

She doesn't turn around as I grab the soap myself and start working my cock. Looking at her ass helps me along. I can only imagine sliding my cock between her ass cheeks before burying it in her ass. She's perfect for this fantasy. I grab my balls with my other hand and enjoy the soapy slide of my hand. It would be nice to step closer and release over her backside, but I resist. I haven't shot a wad this fast in years.

"You want the soap?" I ask after my balls empty.

"You're kidding me, right?" she grumbles and looks over her shoulder at my hand with the soap in it.

"Please yourself, then. I can't promise a shower every day, so take advantage while you can." She bends a little and picks up the shampoo bottle. My dick gives another fucking twitch. She's killing me.

I reach above her head and adjust the showerhead so it's a little behind her. I quickly wash myself and don't put my hand back on my cock or we'll be in here even longer. I finish and step from the shower. When the water goes off, I hand a towel to Sofia and she wraps herself in it leaving her hair dripping. I toss her my damp towel to use on her hair before walking out of the bathroom. From the small closet beside the bathroom door, I grab her travel bag and carry it into her. I searched it and found nothing she could use as a weapon.

"If you have shorts, put them on. This place only gets hotter throughout the day and you have a lot of work to do." I watch her fight back an unpleasant retort. It's impressive that she actually manages to hold it in. I'm purposely pushing all her buttons this morning. The clubhouse should be mostly empty. If she's going to throw a fit, I want her doing it when no one else is around so I don't need to prove I can control her. She's still in a precarious position and so am I for that matter. If the brothers don't think I can handle her, we're both fucked.

"Could I start by cleaning the shower? It's growing antibiotics and I prefer mine in a pill."

I laugh deep and hard. "I'll feed you first," I finally say. "Get dressed and then we'll go scrounge some food."

I leave her in the bathroom and dig some clothes out of the bag I haven't had time to unpack. She won't be cleaning just the bathroom, she'll tackle this entire room too. I whistle as I dress. If I'm lucky, no one will try to kill me today. If I'm unlucky, I'll die.

# 14

*Sofia*

**I couldn't believe when** he left me alone in the room last night. He walked out and locked the door before I knew what was happening. My pussy throbbed for relief and I couldn't help giving it some. I finger-fucked my pussy while thinking about Dagger doing the dirty. And I mean very dirty. My imagination is always better than actual sex. And fuck, I had two orgasms and was still unsatisfied when I finally passed out.

When Dagger entered the hot, airless room this morning, I was dead to the world. It was too sweltering in the room to care that I was naked. Not that Dagger hasn't seen the goods. I'm not exactly modest at the best of times. If Dagger thinks he can humiliate me by keeping me naked, he has the wrong woman. I can handle whatever he throws my way.

Today is hotter than yesterday, which proves hell actually exists. I was excited to take a shower until Dagger joined me. Fuck, how do I resist him now? Watching him jack himself before I turned around will stay imprinted on my brain forever. The man has no modesty whatsoever, and now I'm as horny as I was before jillin' last night.

I brought exactly one pair of shorts, so I'm basically screwed when it comes to staying cool in this hot tin can the Crows call a clubhouse. In my skimpy red workout shorts, gray tank top, and athletic shoes, I follow Dagger to the kitchen. One of the guys is passed out on the floor in the corner of the front room, but other than that, the place appears empty. At least the ceiling fans in this part of the clubhouse keep the air circulating.

Dagger whistles when he enters the kitchen. "I'm impressed," he says as he looks around.

"Why? You know cleaning is the staple job for us Latina women, right?"

He throws his head back and laughs. The sound rolls down my spine, tingles my ass, and zips to my pussy. I'm not crazy about the wet panties I'm beginning my day with. He's wearing a T-shirt for a change and it's almost worse than bare skin. The dark blue material stretches over the swells and valleys of his chest and back. His jeans hang loosely at his waist and stay up with the help of his belt. I have no idea how they still manage to show off his ass.

I need some privacy to relieve the ache between my thighs and I don't see that happening. He's in such a damn good mood because his jizz took a trip down the shower drain while my frustration is at nuclear levels. Now that I've seen his larger-than-life cock, I'm caught between lust and hatred. I remember fucking a guy a few years ago because he had great arms. Unfortunately, his dick didn't live up to his biceps. Dagger's cock far outdoes his body. And, if I'm honest, everything about him does it for me. How a piece of shit skinhead can turn me into a hot wet mess is beyond me. It's my fucked up internal wiring, must be.

Dagger ambles over and opens the refrigerator. The smell knocks us both back.

"Does anyone in this place ever clean anything?" I grumble loudly.

He shakes his head. "Not that I can tell. I rarely came into the kitchen and you've seen the clubhouse and my room. How about we go out for breakfast?"

Is he serious? No way will I pass up an opportunity to escape if he gives it to me.

A knowing look enters his eyes and he steps into my space. His hands go to my hips and, I shit you not, he lifts me off my feet and plops my ass on the counter. He moves between my legs and leans close so his eyes are inches from mine. "If you run or make a scene, it will fall on Red. I've done everything I can to keep you both alive. You and I both know you don't want Red to suffer because of you. If you behave, you will at least have the run of this place and the occasional outing on my bike. If not, I'll keep you under lock and key in that hot, stuffy room." He reaches up, takes a piece of my hair between his fingers, and gives it a slight tug. "We clear?" His blue eyes are so close I can see dark steely flecks in them and I have no doubt he means what he says.

"Yes," I answer honestly. This doesn't mean I won't take the first opportunity and run with Red. I won't endanger her, though, and he knows that, damn him.

His hand slides to my jaw and he slowly runs one finger over my skin. "There will be a man that I trust on you at all times. Bottom line, watching you takes a good man away from the tasks I need done. Don't fuck with me, princess."

Our eyes remain locked as I whisper, "Would my promise be enough so your man can get his work done?" What would he do if I kissed him? Does my Latina blood keep him away? Would he spit and wipe his mouth if I did exactly what I want to? Maybe I'm only good enough to *look* at naked.

His fingers move to the back of my neck and his voice drops to match mine. "You don't get me, princess. My man won't be there to keep you from running. His job is to keep my brothers from killing you."

I've done this to myself. Put myself under the roof with a bunch of bigoted outlaws who hate me. Not just because I pulled a gun on their boss but because of my skin color. The realization turns my stomach sour. "I get it," I say with more attitude than I intend.

Dagger's nostrils flare. I can smell the soap along with the underlying scent that is all him. Do I have the same effect on him? I want to fuck him so bad it hurts. My thoughts turn to his cock—his large fingers sliding over his cock to be exact.

Dagger breaks the spell by lifting me down. "Come on, princess, let's go grab some food," he says casually.

I watch him stride away and take a few deep breaths to control myself. He has me tied in knots and I have no idea how to handle him. I slowly follow him back to his bedroom.

"Put some jeans on. You don't ride with me in shorts," he says over his shoulder as he tosses my travel bag onto the bed, where it bounces. Should I tell him I've never been on a motorcycle? Admitting weakness isn't exactly my strong suit, so I keep my mouth shut. Like everything else in my life, bravado will get me through.

After I've changed, Dagger leads me outside to his bike. The row of them I noticed yesterday is gone and now there are only three. Dagger's bike has seen better days. The layer of dust on the bike doesn't surprise me but the dented frame does.

"Accident a few days ago and had to do a quick fix-it job yesterday," he says when I stand there staring at the bike.

Great, that's all I need to hear. "What about helmets?" I ask him after looking around and seeing none.

His lips tip up in a half smile. "Arizona is a no-helmet state. I wear one when I go into the city. We won't go far and you'll be safe, no worries."

He must be joking. "You just told me you crashed. Is that what happened to your hand too?"

The smile disappears. "I was forced off the road by some guys in Phoenix. We worked it out and they helped me rescue the baby who Fox was planning to sell. I'm not happy about my bike or my hand but that's what it took to get the job done."

"Is she safe?"

"She's with her aunt. That's all I know right now. At least Kiley has a chance."

Hell, I can't like this man. Want to fuck him, yes. Like him, no.

Dagger grabs sunglasses out of a bag on the side of his bike. He already has a pair on, which he grabbed from his room. He hands the glasses to me and I put them on. He places his leg over the bike and turns to me. I take his offered hand and sling my leg over the back. I grab him tightly around the waist and feel a rumble of laughter in his abs. I hold on as he revs the engine and takes off.

"Never ridden, have you?" he yells over the too loud motor.

Damnit, how did he know? I don't answer because I'm too nervous to give him any shit. He keeps his speed down until we turn north on 87 and then he takes off.

"Hang on, princess," he yells.

I'm really beginning to hate that name.

# 15

*Dax*

**The fear in her** eyes surprised me before we took off on the bike.
It's the first time I've noticed anything besides anger, disgust, or
desire shining in those dark orbs. She's a tough cookie, and I'm
learning her eyes hold the answers. I don't think she's accustomed to
hiding her feelings and the last twenty-four hours haven't been easy
on her. I'm aware from Red's story that her fists do a lot of her
talking. She fascinates me while keeping my fucking dick hard. It's
not a combination I'm accustomed to.

We're heading to Payson early on a Sunday morning and the
road is mostly empty. Sofia's arms locked tightly around my waist
make the ride sweeter. It's been a long time since I've ridden with a
babe on the back. It wasn't something Savannah cared for. I gain
speed and enjoy the wind against my face and the roar of the engine.
I allow my thoughts to settle on the club. There's nothing like
working out problems while flying free.

The brothers need to take a ride next weekend. Sometimes
talking and fighting don't resolve what a club ride can. As corny as it
sounds, riding free brings a sense of harmony. I bought this bike
before I married Savannah. It was the only thing Savannah's father
didn't fight me to keep when I got out of prison. I have a picture of
her, which I keep in my wallet, our wedding rings, and this bike.
That first year after leaving a cell I couldn't so much as ride in a car.
Too confined. I needed open air without a cage. Then I hooked up
with the Crows and because we all had similar backgrounds, they
understood.

Definitely a ride next weekend.

The drug buy will take place Friday night. We're in a sticky situation with the people delivering the drugs. They dealt with Fox and his Sergeant at Arms, Clutch. We need to get out from under them and I can only hope the plan we decided on will work. I'll worry about it later. Right now I'm enjoying the freedom I missed so much while I was behind bars. I'd rather die than go back.

Sofia barely moves and that makes me smile, until a bug flies into my mouth. Even eating bugs is better than prison. It's a twenty-minute ride to Payson. We hit the Sonic on the right side of the highway by the casino. I roll the bike under the covered parking and turn off the engine. "We can take it back to the club or eat on the patio," I tell her.

"Patio, please," she says in a shaky voice. She's trembling when I take her hand and help her off the bike. She won't look at me. I squeeze her fingers and pretend I have no idea how terrified she was to ride.

I'll admit I'm wary about having her in public. I don't need trouble with the cops. I'm not wearing my colors or carrying my gun. As an ex-con, I'm a prohibited possessor of a gun. Sofia needs to keep it casual and I'm hoping my threat against Red will do the trick. Even so, I don't see her as someone who cries to the cops. She fucking pointed a gun at me yesterday. She also planned to murder Fox.

We place our order. This isn't exactly how you wine and dine a girl. This is me, though. After seven years of hell inside prison, I'd rather eat fast food whenever possible than sit inside a restaurant. I take a good long look at Sofia.

She takes off the sunglasses and moves a stray piece of hair out of her eyes. "Why are you looking at me like that, *bolillo*?"

"*Bolillo*?"

"Never heard a white slur before?"

I can't help the grin that splits my face. She's always challenging me. "Never heard that particular one, princess." Her eyes are almost black. I'd like to see them burning as I ram my cock into her tight little pussy.

"It means white bread bun."

My laugh is loud in the quiet setting. No one else is sitting outside their vehicle. It's in the low eighties up here in the mountains. Much cooler than Phoenix but still hot enough to stay in the car with the air cranked. "That the best insult you got?"

For the first time, her eyes crinkle with laughter and her lips twitch. "Well there is dog fucker but I'm saving that one."

I think about that before asking, "What the hell does that have to do with being white?"

She bites her lip and I know she's doing her best to keep from smiling. It's so fucking sexy. "Didn't you know that bestiality porn is all done by white dudes?"

I almost spit out my drink. "You shittin' me and how the fuck would you know that? Don't tell me you're into that shit." God, I hope not. My dick was getting a charge out of this conversation and now it's wilting faster than picked daisies.

She innocently blinks her long eyelashes. "No. You may not have noticed but my skin is a nice brown tone. That keeps me from fucking sheep." Her smile breaks through and I want nothing more than to kiss her. No... devour her. "It rather sucks that there aren't more derogatory descriptive white slams," she continues. "Your people have no problem finding terms for anyone without pasty skin."

Her kind, my kind. "Why does there need to be a kind?" I ask because I'm truly interested in her answer.

Her laugh is bitter, the smile disappears, and her voice goes tight. "You're the president of a skinhead motorcycle gang and you have the balls to ask me that?"

I look out over the parking lot and gaze at the desert hills to the south. Another block or two north and pine trees take over. Payson is a mountain town around five thousand feet above sea level. Peach City is at three thousand and it's much hotter. I bring my focus back to Sofia. I've never explained myself to anyone. It's not a pretty story and there are parts that I keep deeply buried. "First: We're a club, not a gang. And second: What do you think would have happened to you yesterday if you tried to kill Fox?" I refuse to call that piece of shit her father.

She shrugs. "I don't know. Hopefully I wouldn't have missed." I hear the resolve in her voice.

"He was a mean son of a bitch and you look nothing like him. Wouldn't have mattered anyway. He'd have killed you. Slit your throat most likely. No chance he would have passed you around to the men because they wouldn't stick their dick in your Latina pussy." She doesn't look angry, just curious, so I continue. "Not that they wouldn't want to. It's a nice pussy," I say trying to lighten the mood. She doesn't look away and her tight expression stays in place. It was a poor joke but I'll admit she flusters me. "The brothers followed Fox because he brought them together and offered protection as long as they lived by his rules. He was no good for them... us. I'm trying to change that. It won't happen overnight. I can't erase years of segregation and hatred in a day or even a week." I clench my teeth and get to the heart of the problem. "You and your vengeance, or whatever you want to call it, almost ruined everything."

Before she can respond, a teenage waitress on roller skates delivers our food. I pay with cash and give her a five dollar tip. Her eyes light up and she thanks me with a shy smile before asking if there's anything else we need before she heads back in.

Sofia takes a long sip from her drink and rips into her egg sandwich. "Change how?" she asks after two bites.

I enjoy the taste of my sandwich before answering. "The brothers came out of the prison system. It's a rough place and if you don't have protection inside, your life isn't worth shit. I know because I tried to play that game. Had the shit beat out of me, so I hooked up with the Aryans." I stop talking for a moment and give myself time to decide how much to say. I gaze back at the desert hills and continue. "Coming into the real world when you get out isn't easy. If you have no support, you end up back inside. Fox offered a sense of family." I give a disgusted laugh and fix my gaze on Sofia. "Before I knew what happened, I was doing fucked up shit for him. Once you're in that deep, you're in." I so badly want her to understand. "Fox was getting crazier every day. If it wasn't me who took him out, someone else would have. Doesn't mean it would have been better for the men of the club." I take another bite and swallow it down with a gulp of soda. "I want better. All the brothers do. Some are still mixed up with the ethnic shit from prison. Maybe they'll change, maybe they won't. The rest don't really give a fuck. Families are diverse in their thinking and if we have each other's backs and keep the club out of trouble, we can build something solid."

She rolls her eyes and looks at me like I'm stupid. "That's easy to say but who the fuck do you have doing the cleaning? A wetback spic," she bites out. "I was born in this country. I'm as

American as you and your brothers, but I'll always be a second-class citizen to the likes of you."

I steal one of her tater tots because I'm cruel that way; I don't rise to the bait. "We have three *white* women heading deep into withdrawals. They're usually the ones who clean and every so often cook. They stay in a single-wide behind the clubhouse. Red's in charge of them until they're out of the woods or decide to leave and go back on the drugs."

Her expression changes only slightly. "Those women never cleaned any part of that club and if you think they did, you're dumber than most Bubbas."

At least I understand this insult. I enjoy her spirit and sparring with her. And she's correct about the cleaning aspect of the women's job. I steal another tater tot.

"Eat your own," she huffs.

I give her my best *who me* smile and take a drink of soda. "I know the whores cleaned things up every once in a while after Fox would finally put his foot down. They're junkies. They do the minimum required for their next fix and most of that was on their backs or knees. They can get off the drugs or get out—"

"You call them whores and talk about them servicing your club like they're some form of animal and you expect them to do what you say," she interrupts. "Has it ever occurred to you to offer them respect?"

My food is gone and I look longingly at her tater tots again. She pushes them toward me.          I finish them off quickly and try to explain to an outsider. "Club whores serve the brothers. They have no problem with the distinction or they wouldn't be there to begin with. In most clubs they want to snag one of the brothers and become an old lady. That's not the way things have been with Fox in charge. They whore for drugs. The men treat them like shit and the guys who have old ladies seldom brought those women around. Again, I plan to change that. Red's now Curly Sue's old lady and I think she has what it takes to put her foot down and keep the *ladies* in line."

Sofia sips her drink and stares off into the same hills I looked at a few minutes ago. "Do you plan to ever allow me to leave or are you just extending my life expectancy by a few weeks?"

I rest my hand on hers. She doesn't pull away. Her skin is so damned soft in contrast to mine. "Whether you believe it or not, I fought for you, princess. These men don't want to kill a woman, but they have a strict sense of loyalty to the club and none of them plans to return to prison. You're a threat. I won't make promises I can't keep but I will do my damnedest to make sure you survive."

She stares down at our hands before raising her gaze to mine. "What about you? I know you could get me out of here if you wanted to. I'll never say a word. Hell, I planned to kill Frank and then I pointed the gun at you. I can't tell anyone the truth."

If only it were that simple. "You interfere with the club, you pay a penalty," I tell her. "I also won't risk what I'm trying to build."

Her eyes are direct when she throws her next question at me. "Am I one of the whores or is my Latina blood too much for your *brothers* to handle?"

This shouldn't piss me off but it does. I don't want to think of her spreading her legs for anyone but me. "Is that what you want? There are plenty of *brothers* who will take you up on the offer now that Fox isn't in charge. If you have the itch to share that pussy, be my guest. There's always a price for everything in life and maybe you're even better on your back than you are at cleaning." I'm surprised she doesn't slap me. Her hands clench into fists and I know she wants to.

"You're a dick, you know that, dog fucker."

# 16

*Sofia*

**I'm fuming. What the** hell did he expect me to think? I'd rather have it spelled out than worry about whose bed I'm sleeping in each night or, better yet, who I'm blowing at the bar. I've spent my life facing threats and not hiding. Asshole.

I'm on the bike again and I'm holding on for dear life. He's pissed off and flying like the wind back to the clubhouse. I keep my eyes closed as he takes the sharp curves through the hills without slowing. The hot, dry air hits my face and there's nothing pleasant about the ride.

*There's always a price.* The words rumble through my head. What is my price?

The pathetic fact is that I want Dagger. Down and fucking dirty. Want. Him. Would I whore for the club? Not a chance in hell unless they rape me. I was stupid not to think of that possibility when I set out on this mad journey for vengeance. My life has been a fucked up ride from the get-go. Just once I want to be happy. Live a quiet life without anger impeding on everything I do.

Red is paying the price for my fuck ups now. Will she leave with me if given the chance? Dagger said she's an old lady and will be handling the other women. Why has she stayed this long? I can't leave if she'll take the heat.

This is why Dagger was willing to bring me with him today. He knows I won't endanger Red—she's my weakness. I have two choices: Live with what they will do to Red or settle in while I figure out what the fuck I want to do with my life. When I face facts, I have nowhere else to go. Joey Jay would take me in but I'd need to grovel. I'm not the same person who left Florida. Truthfully, I don't know who the fuck I am at all.

We pull up to the clubhouse and there are two additional bikes parked out front. Dagger isn't worried. He casually helps me off his bike, takes the sunglasses I hand him, and stashes them back in the bike's bag. All of this without meeting my eyes. Yeah, he's still pissed off, but so am I.

Skull walks outside and greets Dagger with a manshake. "You good?" Skull asks him while giving me a side look.

Dagger grunts before replying. "Went to get some food. We need to stock this place with more booze and definitely something to eat."

"I can leave Vamp here and take the truck into the city. Shopping's not my strong suit, though," Skull replies.

I made my decision on the back of Dagger's bike and I might as well get started. "I know what to buy to stock a kitchen."

Both men turn and stare at me.

"She did good in Payson," Dagger says grudgingly.

"My old lady's working extra hours to make up for time she missed while we took care of business," Skull says to Dagger and then looks at me. "If you can stock a kitchen, I can stock a bar."

Dagger stands silently by as I focus on Skull. "I'm ready whenever you are," I offer.

"Let's do it." Skull turns and walks around the outside of the clubhouse. I follow. I can't resist looking at Dagger before I take the final turn around the corner. He hasn't removed his dark glasses, so I can't see his eyes. Why the hell do I care that I'm leaving him when we're both angry? Getting away for a short time will do me good. I don't think straight at the best of times, but, hell, Dagger fries my brain.

I almost trip over a tire, so I turn my attention to where I'm placing my feet. There's a lot of junk behind the clubhouse. I guess the great MC cleanup didn't make it this far. The truck Skull leads me to is as dilapidated as the house. I'm surprised when it starts up immediately. My car is parked next to the truck, and I ignore it.

"Seat belt," Skull says.

I find that funny. He rides a motorcycle with no helmet and forces me to buckle up?

"It's the law," he adds by way of explanation.

That's even funnier. I don't start laughing, though. If I do, tears might take over. I refuse to show weakness in front of any of these men and I'd like to keep it that way.

Skull turns the music up loud signaling that this isn't a chat session. Good, I don't feel like deciphering the brain of another skinhead. The music he plays is old country and the twang grates on my nerves. How can anyone listen to this shit? I sit back in the seat and close my eyes. It's hot and the farther south we head, the hotter it gets. I should have changed into my shorts.

Skull takes me to a warehouse store to shop. It has everything in bulk, including fresh produce. He doesn't bat an eye as I fill the massive cart. He has his own for alcohol. He buys hard liquor and beer. Soda seems to be his mixer of choice and he buys plenty of that too.

I buy six huge bags of tortilla chips for snacks. I also buy what I need to make a vat of salsa. These white boys need to learn something about good, authentic Mexican food.

I pile the cart as high as I can and Skull doesn't stop me. I don't know why but my thoughts turn to Dagger's room and the condition of the sheets on his mussed up bed. "Would you mind if I get new sheets for Dagger's bed?" I ask before I think about how that sounds.

Skull rubs his chin through his gray beard. "Get sets for the other two rooms too. All three beds are the same size and I doubt if any are free of holes the size of Camelback Mountain."

I grab three sets and stack them in his cart. We head to the register and Skull pulls out the largest roll of one hundred dollar bills I've ever seen. I guess I didn't need to worry about how much we bought.

He fills up the truck with gas on the way out of town. I'm hot and cranky when he turns the music on again. "Please no," I groan while covering my ears.

"Driver chooses music, princess."

Not him too. "My name is Sofia."

"Whatever you say, princess."

I look out the window and stew. I can't very well punch him in the face while he's driving. Finally, we pull up in front of the clubhouse. I jump out before the truck stops rolling. Quiet people drive me crazy. Quiet people who listen to shit music more so. I notice additional bikes as I storm into the club. It's about ten degrees cooler inside, which isn't saying much. Dagger isn't in the front room. I storm past the men and head down the hallway to find him. I enter his bedroom and stop cold. The room is actually clean. Dagger is placing his clothes in the battered dresser on the right side of the room.

"You cleaned it," I say in astonishment as I look around the room.

"Needed cleaning," he replies.

I look at the bed. The top sheet is pulled up with several glaring holes showing. "I bought sheets."

"Good thing. These need to go to the nearest garbage. I'll toss 'em if you want to put the new ones on."

I'm talking about sheets for his bed and it's obviously gone over his head. I decide to keep things calm and stop thinking about fucking this man. Yeah right, like that's gonna happen. "I can't believe you didn't make me clean the room."

He straightens from placing items in the bottom drawer. "You went shopping. Hate to shop, so I cleaned. Don't worry, though. You got bar duty and cleanup tonight."

"It's Sunday."

He leans against the dresser and gives me a killer smile. "The brothers don't care. Only church they attend are the meetings we have here. No praying goes on at our meetings and we don't sing no stupid hymns." He looks over my shoulder and then back at me. "Where's Skull?"

"I couldn't take his damn music, so I left him to unload by himself."

Dagger laughs. I like it. "Change into some shorts and we'll both go help. I'm not fond of his music either but driver's choice."

"Is that a motorcycle *club* rule?"

"Nope, that's the driver's code," he says with a bigger grin.

Ignoring the effect he has on me is nearly impossible. My nipples are super charged whenever he's around. I grab my bag and enter the bathroom, closing the door behind me. Stupid really. He's seen it all and maybe I should keep reminding him what he's missing. Hell, I never thought sexual rejection could bother me, so I stay put. I remove my jeans and tee and stare into the mirror. I'm not a small girl, but I'm toned muscle from head to toe. I've always been proud of my body and worked hard to get it. I decide to put on my one and only sexy bra. It's lavender with more lace than material to hold my breasts in. I don't have matching panties, so I keep the black ones on. I pull up the red shorts and add a skimpy white tank that shows off the bra. I have the goods and plan on working them to see if I can get macho man out there to crack.

He's waiting for me when I walk out. I swear a low growl comes from his throat before he turns and storms out of the room. I follow like a good little Latina and can't help my grin.

We stack boxes on every available counter along with the small table pushed up against the side wall in the kitchen. When there's no more room, we stack on the floor. When we're finished, Skull, Dagger, and two other guys I don't know head back into the front room. Rufus, my wet-behind-the-ears bodyguard, is the only one who stays behind. I fill the sink with dish liquid and add some bleach. I grab the plastic garbage container and move it to the refrigerator. I start empting everything from the interior and try to keep from spilling my guts while doing it.

"Can you take the garbage out for me so I can fill it again?" I ask when the trash can is filled to the brim.

He stares at me for a minute before answering. "Follow me. My instructions are to keep you in sight at all times."

Oh, really! "What the hell happens when I need to pee?" I snap.

"Dagger takes care of that. If he ain't here, the door stays open."

I shouldn't have asked. "Oh for fuck's sake," I grumble. I'll deal with the peeing problem with Dagger. I haven't forgiven him for watching me piss yesterday and I'll be damned if some funky kid watches. This Latina pussy is way more than he can handle.

I follow him out back through the door at the rear of the kitchen. The trailer where the women are looks abandoned. A large electric cooler is propped on a wooden table and I guess it filters air inside. I want to check on Red so bad. We head back to the kitchen and I fill the trash can halfway adding a few contents from the freezer. The trash can smells too bad to keep it in the kitchen, so we walk back outside to dump it.

I exhale with relief when I see Red. She's leaning against the trailer smoking a cigarette. Her face is bandaged, but otherwise she appears okay. I walk in her direction and Rufus grabs my arm. "No," he says.

"What the hell do you mean, no?" I yank my arm away and turn back to the trailer. Red's cigarette is smoking on the ground and she's closing the door behind her. What the fuck?

"Prez says to keep the two of you apart. Don't get Red in trouble."

I've managed to keep myself under control for most of the day and now this little bleach boy is about to make me lose my shit. I suck in air as slowly as possible to gain control. I march back inside the clubhouse and wash the refrigerator out. I ignore the bleach fumes making my eyes burn and scrub until it's spotless. I begin unpacking the items that need to stay cold. Rufus opens a door past the refrigerator. It's a closet size pantry with enough shelves to hold the dry goods.

I've worked harder than this before. So why am I so exhausted? I wipe sweat from my brow and wish I had some way to pull up my hair. I grab a clean glass and drink down tap water, which is foul-tasting. I don't say a word to Rufus when the glass is empty; I just walk to the front room. More club members have shown up.

Dagger strides over to me with a beer in hand. "You got bar duty, princess."

I turn on my heel and head behind the bar being sure to sway my hips just for him. There's a fridge back here and when I open it, I see that it's at least cleaner than the other one was before I took bleach to it. I grab a beer and untwist the cap. The damn cap burns my hand but I don't show it. Several of the men are watching me. Dagger has a strange look on his face. He tips his beer to me when I take my first drink. I ignore him and turn to bar duty.

There are cases of beer and pop under the counter. The newly bought hard liquor is lined up against the back wall. There's a club emblem on that same wall above the bottles. It's the same one the club members wear on their vests. It's actually pretty damn cool, but fuck if I tell any of them that. It's a crow on motorcycle handlebars with two skulls in front. Desert Crows is written on a banner across the top. The design is in a black circle. It looks ominous, which is what the person who designed it was going for.

Rock music, thank God, gets louder and I shuffle beers and drinks when the guys approach the bar.

"Beer," one of the guys says. No please or thank you after I hand it to him. Another has me make him a rum and Coke. I do it all without saying a word. It doesn't seem to bother the guys. Rufus is smart enough to walk behind the bar and grab his own beer. I give him the evil eye and he snubs it.

Skull strides in followed by a woman. She's around his age, has huge hair, and wears a lot of makeup. They're carrying stacks of pizza boxes. Thank God, I'm starving. I'm guessing the woman is a whore, via Dagger's explanation. She gives me a strange look and then proceeds to ignore me. "Hey, princess, bring two beers over here," Skull shouts louder than he needs to. The damn music he listens to has damaged his hearing, I know it.

I grab as many beers as I can hold and carry them out to the tables. I'm being a good little Mexican worker. I am, really. I hand Skull two beers and notice the man across from him has an almost empty bottle in front of him. I walk around and set one of the bottles next to him.

I'm stunned when he grabs my hand in an iron grip and squeezes. "If I want a damn beer, I'll ask. Stay the fuck away from me." His grip goes from painful to excruciating and I literally see red. I've had enough. From country music, to an aching pussy, to cleaning and serving ungrateful assholes, my temper shoots from hot to sizzle in point two seconds. I swing the two beers in my other hand with the intent of de-braining him. He leaps out of his chair and takes the hit solidly on the shoulder. He still has hold of my hand and he twists it painfully and forces me to my knees. "You fucking bitch," he says and keeps twisting. He's intent on breaking my arm, and I'm just about to take his legs out from under him.

"That's enough, Bear. I'll handle it." Dagger's voice is low and clipped.

"The only way to handle it is to kill her ass and you know it. You've practically given her free run of the place. She's too dangerous to keep around." He at least loosens his grip as he yells at Dagger.

Everyone has stopped partying and they're staring. Taking this motherfucker down won't earn me any brownie points. My nostrils flare as I breathe in and do everything I can to control myself.

Dagger jerks me up off the floor, which doesn't help, and pushes me slightly away. "It's done, Bear. We've had this talk and I'm not repeating myself."

"She tried to hit me with beer bottles. What the fuck you gonna do about that?" he spits.

"I said I'll handle it."

"She needs to learn respect. If not from you, I'll beat it into her."

Dagger moves so fast I almost fall backward. He grabs the front of Bear's shirt and gets into his face. "You touch her and you'll deal with me. You feel me?"

"Fuck, Dagger, this is bullshit."

"Do. You. Feel. Me?"

Bear steps back and Dagger releases him. He doesn't wait for Bear to give an affirmative answer. He grabs me and pulls me behind him. He keeps a tight hold on my wrist as he marches from the room. I can barely keep up.

This won't be pretty.

# 17

*Dax*

**Her insolence blasts me**. If looks could kill, as they say. She has no idea what I've risked to keep her alive or that the time has come for her to pay up. Nothing in this fucked up world is free, and I'm tired of watching her sassy breasts and the sway of her tight ass without taking her up on the offer. I can't allow her to leave, it's too dangerous, and in order for her to stay with the club, she needs to be part of it.

Her skimpy shirt clings to her and does nothing to hide the bit of lace she's wearing to push out her breasts. There's sweat on her brow and her dark hair is wild with wisps sticking up all over the place. She must read something in my eyes because she steps back.

"Not a good idea, princess," I say as I reach above her head and close the bedroom door behind her. I pull her closer and she pushes against my chest, which does absolutely nothing. I'm bigger and stronger and so are my brothers. That's another lesson she needs to learn. My right hand slides up her back until I grab a nice chuck of hair at her neckline. It's time to set the record straight and teach her her place.

"You have one chance and one chance only to choose who you belong to—my brothers or me. They'll share you like a club whore until there's nothing left. I'll fuck you the same way, but I don't share." I roughly pull her head back.

There's fire in her brown eyes—fury and desire mixed. Her voice holds only fury when she says, "That's my choice? I can be gang raped or fucked by you?"

I have no idea why I'm always pushing her. I'll admit the fire in her dark eyes turns me the fuck on. "I haven't made up my mind if your pussy is worth the trouble or not. If you choose me, we'll start with a blow job."

Her right palm slams upward between us. She tries to jam it into my chin. I jerk my head back just in time. I twist her around so her back is to my chest while keeping a tight hold on her hair. My left hand slides up until I'm holding one firm breast. I squeeze until she groans.

"Like that, do you?"

"Fuck you, Dagger." She's breathing hard. She wants me but thinks it will be on her terms. There's no doubt I want her, and I press my cock against her ass so she knows how bad.

"Am I your choice or my men? It's time to decide, princess."

She's breathing heavily and before she answers, she releases a low growly sound. "You... you fucking piece of shit. Go ahead and fuck me. You've wanted to since the first time you saw my Latina ass." She stops fighting me physically and I'm practically holding up her limp body. She's right, I have wanted her since I saw her step out of her car and point the gun at me. We're both fucking insane.

I whisper against her throat, "Knees." She always smells fucking incredible. "You'll suck me off and make it fucking good or I'll drag you out naked and let my men enjoy you." I have no idea what's come over me.

Her breath hitches. She fucking likes it. I loosen my grip on her hair and lower my hand from her breast. She turns in my arms until our eyes meet. The fire in her eyes is hotter than ever.

Very slowly she sinks to her knees. Why do I want to fuck this woman until she screams my name and want to break her at the same time? The sight of her on her knees turns my already hard dick to stone.

She jerkily works on my belt. She continues staring at me until the buckle falls loose and then she drops her eyes to her task. Her hands actually tremble as she tackles the button and zipper on my jeans. I should stop what's about to happen. Too. Damn. Bad.

While she concentrates, her tongue comes out and she moistens her red, fuckable lips. My cock jumps and I almost explode before she even wraps her mouth around me. My breathing accelerates and I swear I couldn't talk if I wanted to. She pulls back my jeans and they slip over my ass. She tugs down the front of my tight boxers and my cock springs free. Her warm breath slides over me and it's all I can do not to grab her hair and force my cock down her throat.

Her gaze lifts to mine and her tongue comes out. Just the tip slides up the length of my cock from balls to tip. I suck air into my lungs. It's been too long since I've wanted something this bad and fuck if I allow it to end in the first few seconds. She rises higher on her knees and her lips slip over the head.

I'm actually surprised she gave in this easily. A thought occurs in my clouded brain, and I pull her hair back so my dick slips from her mouth. "If you fucking bite me, I'll knock out your teeth."

She rolls her eyes and from this vantage point it's sexy as fuck. She slides her tongue out and licks me. My fingers slip from her hair and she takes me in her mouth again. Her hot, slippery, fucking mouth. I can't fight the low groan that escapes my throat.

She cups my balls and adds a healthy squeeze. I close my eyes for a few seconds as her lips, tongue, and yes the slight pressure of teeth pull me down the path of no return. My hands move to either side of her head and I adjust her speed. She's taking me slow and deep, but I need fast. My balls tighten as saliva runs from the corner of her mouth. She's watching me with a look of satisfaction in her all-knowing eyes.

I groan again as the first wave of cum leaves my dick. Too bad if she's not the swallowing type because I'm holding her head and giving her no choice. She swallows down what she can. My cum mixes with the saliva and drips onto the front of her shirt.

Fuck yes, this is what I need.

Sofia is part heaven and part hell and I want all of her.

## 18

*Sofia*

**Men are so fucking** easy and Dagger is no different. I rise slowly and bring the waist of his boxers and jeans up over his ass. I don't remove my eyes from his as I buckle him up. He reaches down to my face and rubs his finger from my chin up to my bottom lip. His finger goes to his lips.

Fuck, that's hot.

"Are we going back out there?" I ask sweetly. I'm so turned on it hurts. Won't work for my plan, though, so I try not to convey that my pussy needs action.

"Yeah," he says with sleepy eyes and a satisfied look on his face. "There will be pizza left over and you can have some after the brothers finish."

That's a direct shot to my pussy and not in a good way. I seethe and do my best to keep the fire out of my eyes. I follow Dagger back into the main room and try to look contrite as the guys watch me head back to the bar. I grab two more beers and carry them to Skull and the woman who finished off the last two I carried over. I wonder if they'll pass her old ass around tonight seeing as the other whores are incapacitated.

I put the beers down between Skull and the woman and take a slight detour back to the bar so I can walk behind the man who grabbed my arm earlier. It's so simple really. I grab Dagger's knife from where I stashed it in the back of my shorts. I have it around Bear's throat pressing against his windpipe before anyone guesses my intentions. Bear's entire body stiffens and all talk in the room ceases.

Dagger's knife is as sharp as I expected and I'm drawing blood.

"Everyone back off," I say loud enough to be heard over the music. "Bear and I are having a chat and I will slit his throat before anyone stops me." I don't need to look to know Dagger's checking the sheath at his hip. Empty, sucker, and I truly wish I had time to laugh. "So, big boy," I say loudly in Bear's ear, "this is the thing... for as long as I can remember, I planned to kill my father. He fucked my mother over with drugs, whored her out to his friends, and regularly beat the shit out of her. He also killed two innocent babies she carried. They were my blood, completely innocent, and he beat them out of her," I stress my horror with a little added pressure. "I dreamt about holding his severed dick in my hands every day from the time I was young. The very day the shit goes down it's taken away from me."

I'm doing the best I can to control the simmering rage and it's so fucking hard not to end this worthless piece of shit's life. "In steps Dagger, the man who killed my father. I never expected to survive what I planned to do and I made my peace with God before I came here. My life has been shit and I'm one of the meanest bitches you'll ever meet. Believe me, this world wouldn't miss out because I'm not in it. Dagger talked about a different club than the one Fox controlled, so I made the decision to live. I'll cook and clean and fuck your prez. I'll even blow him if he's got the balls to let me near his cock again." A humorless laugh escapes me. "I'm damn good at everything I just listed. You want respect, then you better sure as fuck offer it." My left hand is on his shoulder and I squeeze my nails into his T-shirt to keep myself from slitting his throat. "You. Get. Me?" I use Dagger's turn of phrase with the same emphasis but don't let him answer. "I have two choices right now..." I let that hang for a moment. "I can slit your throat and the men in this room will kill me... or I can get back to work." I remove the knife, palm it, and stab it down into the wooden table between Bear's hands. "Here's your chance, big boy. Kill me and get it over with or let me get back to fucking work."

No one moves. I expect to be tackled, hit up the side of the head, or stabbed by Bear. He slowly slides his hand to the knife and turns slightly, peering over my shoulder. My eyes follow the direction of his gaze. "That must have been one hell of a blow job," he says to Dagger.

Dagger has the bubba look and I'll be damned if it isn't cute on him. Then, he actually smirks. "Best blow job ever."

Bear looks up at me. His voice is deceptively calm for a man who just about met his maker. "You say you can cook?"

"Better than the shit I had last night." I remove my hand from his shoulder and the tension in my back and shoulders ease.

"As long as I don't have fire bombs coming out my ass all night, I'll give it a try."

His gaze travels back to Dagger. "She's just as fucking crazy as you. I hope to God you know what you're doing."

Dagger nods. "I'll stash my knife before fucking her again, that's for damn sure."

The men begin laughing and the woman sitting next to Skull joins in. When it quiets down, she throws an arm around Skull's shoulder. "You asked me earlier if I wanted to move our trailer onto club property and save money. The answer's yes." Skull pulls her close and kisses her. He smiles when he comes up for air. I realize this is an old lady and not one of the whores. God, only one day and I'm picking up the vernacular. She looks at me and stands up. "Come on, sugar, I'll help serve so we can get this party started."

Before I move away, I reach around Bear and grab a slice of pizza from the box beside him. I don't look at Dagger. I'll be damned if I starve while everyone else eats.

"I'm Charley," Skull's woman says when we walk behind the bar. She puts out her hand and I shake it. "You got a set of balls on you, girly, I'll give you that." She picks up a rag and wipes down the top of the bar. "Haven't been here in months. Couldn't stand the place. Skull put his foot down tonight and told me things were changing. I guess he's right and it's about time. I style hair for a living. You have Dagger bring you by when you want a cut and some color."

There's no way I'm hurting her feelings and telling her I like my hair as is, so I just nod while she keeps talking. "Got no kids but wish we did. Getting too old now and I think we're a little selfish. Takes lots of money to raise kids nowadays. Skull says he's quitten' his job and goin' to work on the project Dagger has planned out on the highway. My man says they'll make it work and after things are settled I can cut back my hours at the salon."

I let her speak without interrupting and learn more about the club than I could possibly pick up from Dagger. No wonder Skull doesn't say a lot—Charley never shuts up.

"Bear's nothing but a big teddy. You and him got off on the wrong foot seein' as you tried to blow a hole in Dagger. My man wasn't too happy with you either. These men respect balls, so you'll get along just fine. Not that it would have worked before Dagger took care of Fox." Her expression changes and she looks at me compassionately. "I know you hated him and you have a right. Can't say I'm sorry that son of a bitch is dead."

Again I nod and she doesn't stop rambling. The only break I get is when Dagger brings a box of pizza over and rests it on top of the bar. His knife is back in the sheath. "Eat some more. You're going to need your strength tonight." I can't decipher his expression.

He saunters off and Charley leans in close and whispers, "That man is damn sexy. If I didn't have Skull, I'd do 'em. Expect him to be a little rough tonight after what you pulled. I don't think you'll complain, though. Angry sex can be the best kind."

I open a beer after offering one to Charley. "I'll let you know how it goes."

Her laugh carries across the room and all the men turn. I tip my beer to Dagger. He doesn't tip his back. He's pissed off and trying to control it. I know the feeling.

# 19

*Dax*

**Crazy fucking woman. I** should tan her ass for that little stunt. I can't believe she swiped my knife. Yeah, the blow job was that fucking good. The thought of leaving my handprint on her ass is the only thing that calms me enough to hold my shit together.

I checked on Red around ten. The three women were passed out and Red was standing in front of the trailer smoking a cigarette. She's still pissed at me for keeping her away from Sofia. She wasn't happy when I told her Sofia extended the ban with her knife trick tonight. I walked away before Red finished giving me shit. I drink another beer when I'm inside and imagine Sofia on her hands and knees taking my dick in her ass. I want to hurt her. And I want her to fucking like it. I'm a sick bastard.

The majority of the men start heading home around midnight. Many of them have jobs to go to in the morning. I really appreciate Skull bringing his old lady. We need the women here and not just the whores.

Bear was definitely right in one thing. Sofia is as fucking crazy as I am. She'd make a fine old lady. I stop that thought. You take an old lady because of more than the fact that they're a crazy bitch and make your dick hard. You need to care about them. My cock cares about Sofia, but my brain thinks she may be too much trouble.

Skull and Charley take off and Sofia keeps cleaning tables like it's her favorite thing in the world to do. It's a chance to shake her ass and bounce her breasts is what it is. The few men left are playing cards and might be here for hours. They enjoy the show

Sofia puts on. I finally can't take anymore and grab her when she tries to walk past me. I stand and haul her up and over my shoulder.

"What the fuck, Dagger?" she yells. My hand lands on her ass with a solid thwap. She struggles and yells louder, so I smack her again. The men are laughing as I carry her away.

"Hide the blade, brother," I hear behind me and ignore it. The men will never let me live this one down, and Sofia's lucky she's still alive. I can't believe she won Bear's respect with that stupid stunt.

I toss her on my bed and walk away to slam the door with my foot. "You have ten seconds to get out of that shit you're wearing, roll over, and get your ass in the air," I tell her as I begin tearing off my clothes.

"This, most likely, isn't the best way to begin our relationship," she retorts.

I don't say another word. I pull my riding boots off and slide my pants down after taking my knife from its sheath.

She quickly lifts her arms and pulls her tee over her head. She shimmies around and slides the shorts off after kicking her shoes to the floor. I kneel on the bed and stop her when she reaches around to undo her lace bra. Yeah, lace. Not the sport thing she wore yesterday. I push her back on the bed and move in closer on my knees. I bring the knife down to the front of her chest and turn the blade so the sharp side is up. I slip it beneath the lace at the front of the bra and slice. The fabric separates and her tits swing free.

"You asshole. I only have one other bra," she says throatily. Her eyes are dilated and her breathing erratic. Danger turns this woman the fuck on. She slips that small pointed tongue out and slides it across her upper cherry-red lip.

"Pull that stunt again and you'll stay tied to this bed naked for a week," I tell her while staring at her perfect breasts. I watch as her nipples turn to dark pinpoints and I haven't even touched the damn things.

I grasp her at either side of her waist and flip her over. I slip the matching panties from her ass and leave the cut bra on. My left arm circles beneath her stomach and I pull her to her knees. God, I want that tight ass, and she has no idea what it takes to slide my fingers past it and find her pussy. She's wet and she moans when I slide one finger inside her sweet cunt.

"Oh, God, that feels good," she says on a slow breath.

I'll be damned if I'm giving her pleasure. I line myself up and shove my dick in to the hilt. She gives a sharp cry. I'm big and she's so fucking tight. I rise up and bring her hips with me holding her up with both hands. Her knees are no longer on the bed and I don't give a fuck if this is uncomfortable. She falls to her forearms as I continue driving in and out. She moans again and I release her with one hand and slap her ass before pushing my dick in as far as it goes. That's all it takes and I unleash inside her. The blood pounds in my brain and charges through nerve endings straight to my cock. I bury my face into the hair at her neckline and fill my lungs with her scent. I continue pumping in and out until my balls are empty. I slide out, smack her ass, and collapse on the bed.

Sofia rolls over and tries to grab the knife that I tossed on the side of the bed. I get to it first and throw it across the room.

"You're not leaving me like this. You can't," she grumbles.

I grab her around the waist, roll her, and bring her back to my chest. "Shut the fuck up and get some sleep. You want to get off, you'll work out a proper apology by tomorrow morning and I'll think about it."

"You bastard."

I slide one hand up and pinch her nipple hard. "Go to sleep or you'll be giving me another blow job."

"You put that damn thing near my mouth and I'll fucking bite it off. I don't give a shit about your threat to knock my teeth out."

"Shut up or I'll gag you." I squeeze her nipple again and the damn little bitch likes it. I reach over and turn off the lamp next to the bed before closing my eyes. The smell of her hair and the scent of sex is the last thing I remember before sleep consumes me.

A warm hand wrapped around my dick wakes me up. Sofia is curled at my side and her hand is rubbing along my length in a leisurely fashion. Sun is sliding through the blinds and offering its soft glow to the bed.

"You got an apology for me?" I groan into her hair. It still smells wonderful.

She hesitates before responding. "I'm sorry."

It's said grudgingly and I can't help chuckling. I roll to my back and bring her over me so she's straddling me. I drag her pussy along my chest and then lift her a bit until her knees rest on my shoulders and her hands go flat against the wall. God, her pussy smells fucking good. I don't care that it's sex from last night, I lap my tongue over her folds and inhale.

Her moan is loud in the room and I smile against her cunt. I've always enjoyed eating out a woman. Hers may be the fucking best pussy I've ever tasted. Some men might like a woman washed and shaved. I don't mind the shaving, but God I love the nasty taste of sex dripping from a woman's pussy. I find her clit with my tongue and flick it a few times. She grinds against me telling me exactly want she wants.

"Try another apology, but this time fucking mean it if you want me to suck your clit." I grin against her pussy lips and hope she can't feel it.

"God, I hate you."

My tongue flicks over her again.

"Fuck, I'm sorry. Really sorry," she whines in desperation.

Maybe she is, maybe she isn't. I can't help myself, I want her to come all over my face. I pull her engorged clit between my lips and suck. Her head goes back and she makes wonderful sounds as she cusses and talks dirty.

"Fuck, Dagger, fuck. Slide your finger in my ass, fuck."

That answers that question. I should have fucked her there last night. I push my thumb in. She groans and pants. Her tight little hole latches onto my thumb and I gently bite her clit.

She screams and lets go. Her throat makes a low humming noise. I'll be sure to get her off when she gives me the next blow job. I remove my thumb, sit up, and move her down so her pussy slides over my dick. Fuck, she's tight. Her hands clench my shoulders as I lift her up and down on my cock. I'm rock hard, but I have a little more control than the last few times I've gotten off. I suck one sweet nipple into my mouth and get a small moan for the effort. I keep the pace slow and I can tell she's going to lose it again by the sounds she makes. I switch to the other nipple and give it a bit rougher treatment.

She doesn't shy away from pain. She digs it as much as I enjoy giving it to her. I use every technique I have to hold back my orgasm until her pussy begins pulsing around me. The throaty humming noise starts again and my balls unleash. I think I could fuck this woman around the clock without losing a hard-on for more than a few minutes.

With my hand splayed across her back, I push her down to kiss her for the first time. She covers her mouth and pushes away. "No. I need a toothbrush. I have green shit growing on my teeth, I know it."

I laugh. God, she keeps me on my toes. I just had my face in her dirty pussy and she's worried about bad breath. She's right, though. The least I can do is supply a toothbrush. "I stashed an extra one in the bathroom drawer for you," I say with a smile. She scrambles off me and heads into the bathroom.

"Two minutes and I'm joining you in the shower," I call after her.

I move my hands behind my head and interlock my fingers. The ceiling needs painting as well as the walls. So much shit to do and the bedrooms will be at the bottom of the list. I'm taking a more important step today. I need to find out what permits the county requires in order to build on the property on State Route 87. Sofia can help me if she's willing.

I throw my legs off the bed and get up when I hear the shower turn on. I piss and brush my teeth before jumping in with her. She has a towel over her hair and once again, I'm punched in the gut because it reminds me of Savannah. Two women, so different. There are no comparisons to make but for some reason Sofia makes me think of Savannah.

"You okay, Prez?"

She's staring at me with a look I can't decipher. Who knows the expression I was wearing a moment ago. I've kept thoughts of Savannah at bay for years. Now is not the time for them to creep in. "Make some room so I can wash. We have a lot on our plate today."

"Most men are in a better mood after morning sex," she says and turns her back to me.

I grab her slender waist and pull her back. I kiss her neck and nuzzle the towel at her hairline. "You're right. I'm sorry. I have a lot on my mind. You interested in taking a ride with me into the city today?"

"For what?"

"You need clothes and I thought we could grab you some. Some more sexy panties and a new bra to replace the one I cut off last night to begin with."

"You cleaned the shower and for that I'll go anywhere with you today. Sexy panties are good too."

I laugh against her shoulder. It's been some time since I've laughed as much as I have in the past two days. Sofia's strange, unpredictable ways seem to soften something inside me and I realize I've actually enjoyed sparring with her.

We both wash and we're out the door in thirty. I promise her a bagel from a shop in Fountain Hills, which is near where I'm taking her to shop. I carry two helmets out with me and adjust hers on her head. The head gear makes her even sexier in my book. She acts so fucking tough all the time. Hell, she is tough. I get it. Who the fuck puts a knife to a biker's throat and walks away with respect? She's a package of dynamite set to go off.

"You're not wearing your vest," she points out when I put my hand out to help her on the bike.

"I don't need trouble from the cops. Wearing the vest brings trouble. Sometimes I don't give a shit, but today I have a lot to do and don't want the hassle."

She snuggles up behind me and rests her head against my back. I could get used to this. I open up the throttle when we hit the highway and we head into the city. I take her for bagels and she eats two. I enjoy a woman who puts away food.

Fountain Hills is high-end with some of the most expensive real estate in the valley. There are some discount stores when you get closer to Scottsdale and that's where I head.

"Remember, anything you buy needs to fit in the saddlebags."

"Got it. I don't need much."

I've heard that before. "We'll see."

She picks out two bra and panty sets. I grab two more in the same size, one pink and one red. Sue me, I'm a guy. She buys a few tees and I add a few more that I like. She tries on shorts and we add those too.

"What about those toe sandal things all the women wear?" I ask when she says she's done.

"Flip flops?"

"Yeah, those."

She's smiling when we walk into the shoe section and she grabs a few pairs after trying them on. One set is about three inches high. Funny, but I prefer her in socks.

She still holds me tight around the waist on the trip back but she's more comfortable, her body looser. She also looks out over the landscape. I'll turn her into a biker babe before she knows it.

We're back before noon and drop everything at the clubhouse. I explain that I need her with me when I go to the county offices.

"Why?" she asks after grabbing a bottle of water from behind the bar and downing half of it.

"The club's putting a convenience store out on the highway and I need to find out what permits we need. The property has power and water, it just needs a building."

"That doesn't explain why you need me."

I take the water from her hand and drink the rest. She looks irritated but doesn't say anything. "Navigating shit with the county will be easier if they don't know I'm with the DCMC. Desert Crows Motorcycle Club," I say when she looks clueless at the acronym.

"So you need my Latina ass to keep them from thinking you're the skinhead you look like?"

I run my hand over my head, which I haven't shaved in three days. I'm blond, so it won't show until it's longer and will most likely look like shit for a while. "Yes, something like that."

"Priceless. I think I can handle it."

"I just bet you can."

# 20

*Sofia*

**I think I'm falling** for a skinhead. *It's a fling,* I tell myself. One where I'm forced to stay with a hot guy, clean up his and his gang's shit, and have nasty sex with him. Sounds sick when I think of it that way. The kind of sick that turns me on.

I'm beginning to enjoy riding on the back of his bike too. It's strange the things I think of while sitting behind him with my arms around his waist and my breasts pushing into his back. It's a sense of freedom I've never had before, and as stupid as it seems, I feel safe.

We have helmets on again and it's not quite as wonderful as the freedom of going without one that I had the first time I rode with Dagger. Safety first. That's a joke. I've never played it safe in my life and now that I'm more comfortable on the bike, I want my hair blowing in the wind.

I could leave if I truly wanted to. My car keys are in the top drawer of the dresser. Dagger knows I saw them, but he ignored it. I have no idea what he thinks of me besides being a hole to put his dick in. I shouldn't care but I do. It's only been two days. I'll be the hole for now.

The trip to the county offices takes more than an hour. The desert is beautiful even in the heat. Dagger packs some water bottles in his saddlebags and we pull over halfway and drink one down. Earlier when he took the one from my hand, it shocked me. It was such an intimate thing to do. I don't do intimate. I fuck and walk away. It's strange to be hanging out and doing things with a guy I've fucked. I guess there's a first time for everything.

We hit the county offices and Dagger gets the papers and information he needs. His speech is articulate when he talks to the woman in planning and zoning. He introduces himself as Dax Montgomery and tells her he wants to open a small store and eventually bring in gasoline for four-wheelers. She gives him information from the EPA and the Division of Weights and Measures. I stand by and act as normal as possible. The woman doesn't give us strange looks or act like we're not normal. The chip on my shoulder crumbles a bit at her helpfulness.

Globe, where the county offices are located, is a strange place. It's not the prettiest town I've seen, but when Dagger takes me through the old section of town, I'm enthralled. The old buildings are amazing. They're tall and weathered with shattered windows. Character is all that comes to mind. It's a glimpse of history in an unlikely place.

We eat lunch at a fast food restaurant and sit under an umbrella outside. Dagger seems to have an aversion to eating inside and I keep my mouth shut. It's not like we have a relationship where I can question him about his personal habits. We head back to the clubhouse at what must be the hottest time of day. Sweat forms between us leaving his back and my chest drenched. We pull up to the clubhouse around four in the afternoon.

"How many guys will be here this evening?" I ask after handing Dagger my helmet.

"Depends." He gives me a slightly crooked smile. "You cooking?"

I can't help returning the smile. It's been such a calm day and it's too damn strange to dissect right now. "I was thinking about it," I say hiding the uncertainty that suddenly fills me. I haven't been angry today, not once. It could be a record.

"Make enough for ten and I'll put the word out." He grabs me around the waist and pulls me in close. He kisses me. Hell, does he kiss me. It's the first time our lips touch and I never want it to stop. Kissing isn't exactly my thing. It's another intimacy problem that I don't want to think about right now. His tongue and lips control me and I like it. Maybe too much.

He lifts his head and removes a wisp of hair from my face with his fingers. "Why don't you go ask Red if any of the women care to join us?"

I want to jump up and down for the dumbest reason. The entire ban on speaking to Red was ridiculous and I shouldn't feel elated that he's lifted it. I should kick him in the balls for having it in the first place. Too bad I like his balls. A lot. "I'll head there now and meet you inside." I turn to walk around the building and Dagger pulls me back. His tongue slides between my lips and he circles his arms around me again. We're standing in the hot sun, but I don't care how hot it is. He tastes too damn good. I'm dazed when he lets me go. He turns me around and slaps my ass. Damned if I don't like that too. "Go see Red." He laughs when I moan.

I'm smiling as I walk around the building and head to the old trailer. Fucking smiling! I take the two steps up to the door and knock softly. No one answers, so I knock again a little louder. I lift my hand for another try when the door squeaks and opens a few inches. "You can't be here, Sofia," Red whispers. I can just make out the side of her face. The large bandage still covers her cheek and fuck if it doesn't ruin a perfect day.

"Dagger sent me over," I tell her without the smile I had just a moment ago.

The door flies open and I'm forced to step back. Red's arms wrap around me tightly. "I'm so sorry. I never should have told you all those things. I had no idea you would come out here. I'm so, so sorry." The words spill out in desperate rush.

I'm not exactly the hugging, touchy-feely type. Red gives me no choice, so I hold on. She eventually releases me and drags me inside with one arm hooked over my shoulder. She stares at me in the dim inside light. "Lordy but you're as beautiful as your mother. I've been so worried about you."

The comparison makes me uncomfortable. I look around the small space. It's worse than the clubhouse. "Could we sit down and talk for a few? I need to hurry and start cooking dinner. That's why I came. I wanted to know if you and the other ladies would like to eat at the clubhouse tonight." I say all this in a nervous rush. My mother is not a subject I'm comfortable with. We move to the small table in the kitchen and sit down.

"You're cooking for the club?" she asks while wiping away a few tears and smearing more of her heavy makeup.

I give her a sheepish smile. "I made a deal with Bear. I don't slit his throat and he doesn't behave in a disrespectful manner."

"You shitten' me?" She starts laughing and ends up coughing. It's a smoker's cough and makes it obvious she should quit. Her death, her choice is my motto, so I keep the thought to myself.

"Long story and I don't have time right now to go into details. Dagger said the women in here are going through withdrawals. How are they?" I saw my mother do it too many times to count. It was never pretty.

"Hell, it's been a nightmare, but at least they sleep a lot." She shrugs. "I'm sure you know what it's like." She removes a cigarette from the package on the table and taps it against the table while talking. "They've got the creepy crawlies and don't want anyone near them. I remember back when I went through it. It feels like you're zapped every time something touches your skin. If they decide to stay, the worst will be over in about a week. I'll ask if they want to visit the clubhouse, but I think they'll be more worried the guys will want them to spread their legs."

She's right and it's not a conversation I want to have right now. It only pisses me off more. Men are pieces of shit and while looking at Red's face I'm totally including Dagger in that statement. "I'm sorry about your face, Red. So sorry." Hell, I want to tie Dagger to a chair and give him a matching reminder that he shouldn't fuck with me or someone I care about.

"Ah, this?" She touches the bandage. "Dagger took it easy on me. Fox would have skinned me alive. The prez had no choice, so don't go blamin' him for it."

"Why the fuck not? He's the one who cut you."

Her eyes grow serious. "It's simple, really. I betrayed the club. I survived because half the men were doing the same thing. That's the only way you could survive with Fox as prez. I'm Curly's old lady now, so it's different. Curly claimed me the night this happened. Dagger is a good man. The best this club has had in a long time."

"You planning to stay here?" I ask, though I already know the answer.

"You think I've been here all these years and want to leave now that things are turning around?" She grabs a scrunched up tissue off the table and blows her nose. "I don't want to talk about that. Tell me why you left Florida and came clear out here. You tryin' to get yourself dead?"

I don't understand why she's stayed here this long but again, just like smoking, it's her choice. I stand up and pace a few feet away from the table. "I've always dreamed of killing Frank, you know that. It's all I've ever had, Lorene." I look at her and see pity in her eyes. I wrap my arms around myself. "You told me about that little girl he was planning to sell and I couldn't take anymore. My mom lived in fear of him since the day she got away. He killed her as sure as he killed the babies she carried. I'm twenty-six years old and lived with so much anger all these years."

"And that's why you took a shot at Dagger?" she asks.

I grab my head, which is beginning to ache. "I don't know what came over me. That's what I mean about the anger. It blinds me. What the fuck is wrong with me, Lorene? I've always been this way." I can pretend only so long and even though we never met in person, Lorene has been the only sanity that I can remember in my life.

"Aw, honey." She stands up and places her arms around me again. "I hear you're with Dagger. You deserve someone strong like him to look after you."

She doesn't get it. I don't need anyone looking after me. I'm a head trip with issues that no head shrink could begin to decipher. I can't explain all that to her, though. "Being with Dagger wasn't by choice." Liar, liar pants on fire. I wanted to fuck him. Still want to fuck him. "Getting passed around by the men or sleep with him. What the fuck was I to do?" I have no idea why I'm saying this shit.

Lorene leans away and looks at me. "You keep telling yourself that, Sofia. My man, Curly, says the two of you have the burn." My face heats and she laughs. "Dagger's something else and about as hot as they come. Curly's pretty hot in a middle-aged kind of way, but he don't hold no candle to Dagger. Never heard a woman complain about sleepin' with Dagger either. You can't fool an old horndoggy like me."

"You don't get it. He's forcing me to stay here and phenomenal sex doesn't change that."

"Phenomenal, huh?" Her laughter is so loud I'm surprised she doesn't wake up the women. When it finally dies down, she gives her opinion. "You fucked with the wrong club, girlie. You're paying the price, and from the way I see it, that price hasn't ended with you or me six feet under. We need to appreciate that."

She'll never understand. "I need to go. I'll make extra food and bring it over later. How does that sound?" I say without allowing the anger to swell in my voice. It's not her fault I'm in this predicament.

She walks me outside. I'm halfway to the back door of the clubhouse when she yells, "I'm Red, hun. That's my name here. Lorene no longer exists."

Will I exist when this is over?

I enter the kitchen with a lot on my mind. I'm actually mad that my good mood was ruined. Poking through cupboards for pots and pans calms me somewhat and I begin focusing on cooking. I slice the beef I left in the refrigerator yesterday and place it in two large pans. I'm improvising with everything from pan size to cutlery. The kitchen, including the stove, doesn't have much to offer. I cut up vegetables next, beginning with onions. Dagger walks in and peeks over my shoulder to see what I'm doing.

"I see those aren't real tears," he whispers in my ear and places his hands on my ass.

I'm his possession and it pisses me off when my heartrate jacks up at his touch. "Onions get me every time," I say evenly.

"Whatever you're making already smells good." His breath puffs against my neck and he inhales. "You smell good."

He gently bites my skin and pulls my ass against his hard dick. I wave the knife. "Cooking here. Sharp knife in hand. Man I wanted dead a few days ago is standing too close. Man keeping me prisoner standing too close," I say testily.

He ignores the knife and kisses the place he just bit. "Woman who can cook, clean, and wield a knife. My dick will stay hard until I fuck you."

The thrill of his words pools between my thighs. My body betrays me every time he comes around. The anger dissolves. Hell. "Such a romantic. Leave the kitchen or help."

He slides his hands from my backside. "Believe me, you don't want my help. I can barely make scrambled eggs."

My eyes follow him as he walks to the kitchen door and looks at me over his shoulder. "Thanks for coming with me today, princess."

I'm horny and the best I can do is grunt. He knows exactly what he does to me. I hear his laughter from the other room. I hope his dick stays hard for hours. It will serve him right.

# 21

*Dax*

**It will take a** sizeable chunk of money, but I think we should do this right," I tell the brothers who are gathered around the table. We've moved three tables together so all the men can sit and talk comfortably. I want everyone's input on this. "The permits will take about four weeks if everything runs smoothly. We need to begin ordering building material and have it dropped here so it doesn't disappear. I have several building plans and need everyone to voice an opinion. We need to know exactly what we want in order to get started."

Skull is the first to give his input. "We need a bay for repairs, men and women's bathroom, along with the store area."

I lay several pages of designs on the table and point to the one I like. "I agree. We might want to consider having another section to possibly rent out. It wouldn't cost that much extra and we can leave the inside unfinished for whoever rents it. They can handle the buildout."

"What kind of renter?" Vampire asks.

"I'm not sure. Maybe some kind of fast food place. I think someone will come to us if the space is available."

Curly stands and walks around the table until he can look over my shoulder at the printouts. "You plan to keep this place legitimate?"

I glance at the men. "Eventually, illegal drugs will land us back in prison. Fox scrambled to keep the cops off our back constantly. Laundering the money is a huge problem too. Until we're out of the drug business completely, we need a way to show the money. That way everyone who works the store and garage receives a paycheck. I have some ideas for other ways to make us money too. Right now we need to come to a decision about the building."

Curly picks up the larger building design. "I vote for this one."

The other men give their approval. I'm gathering up the papers when Rufus and Sofia walk out of the kitchen carrying actual dishware. Our usual is paper plates, so this is kind of nice. We pass around the plates and utensils. Rufus and Sofia head back to the kitchen and a few minutes later bring in bowls and platters of food. Fuck does it smell good.

I glance around the tables and watch the men. If the way to a man's heart is through his stomach, Sofia will win each one of them over. Prison food was the worst food I ever tasted. When I got out, I gained ten pounds before I got my appetite under control.

"I'm taking food over to the women and then I'll be back to eat with you. I hope someone's willing to make room for me and Rufus or you can bet your ass I'll spit in the next meal."

Bear stands and grabs another chair from behind him. He places it next to his. "Right here, princess. If this tastes as good as it smells, you have a place by me every night."

They all laugh and I realize Sofia is on her way to being one of us. My heart swells. I told her she almost ruined my plans for the club, but maybe a dose of her Latina smartass is exactly what we need.

She leaves the room with Rufus on her heels. We begin passing around bowls and then start stuffing our faces. The men eat the fajitas and no one complains about the ethnic food. Fox kept everyone in check when it came to anything non-white, even food. Fucking made no sense.

We're halfway done with the meal when Sofia rejoins us. Rufus pulls up his own chair and I make room for him. I don't mind Sofia sitting next to Bear. I need him on my side and the men look up to him. He had a bur up his ass and that's understandable. We're ex-cons and people like to think that PTSD is fully related to military service. Every man here has a horror story about prison. We drink and party hard enjoying every minute we have outside prison walls. Because, I know, each of us can't run fast enough from the fear of going back.

"Food's good," Bear says between bites.

"Good? After the shit you fed me last night, you call this good?" Sofia challenges.

"Better than good," he adds.

She laughs and I enjoy watching her. It's hard to believe she has Fox's blood running through her veins. She looks over at me and flushes. I like that too. If she were sitting next to me, I'd be fingering her pussy. I'm not sure how she knows that, but she picks up her plate and walks over to Rufus. "Switch places. Bear's planning to steal my food and I'd hate to stab him with a fork."

Everyone laughs again. My dick is hard by the time she's sitting beside me. She continues eating with her right hand and slowly slides her left to my crotch.

Dirty girl.

She knew I'd be hard. The guys start talking about the building and it's as if Sofia and I are in our own little world. I lean in and whisper, "Best fucking food I've ever had."

Her fingers tighten on my dick. "I'll give you something better for dessert."

Two more bites are all I can handle. "You aren't that hungry are you?" I ask in desperation. I need to sink balls deep in her hot pussy.

She rests her fork on the side of her plate and stands. The guys look over when I stand and follow her.

"If she fucks as good as she cooks, you're a smart man," AJ calls out.

I flip the guys the finger and follow my hot Latina. I enter the bedroom a few feet behind her and grab her hips bringing her against my body. "Stop right there," I say into her hair.

"You sure are bossy." She moans when I bite her collarbone.

"I know what I want and how I want it. I've been thinking about your tight ass all day. I want to shove my dick in and hear you scream," I whisper between nibbling kisses across her skin. She's salty with sweat and I love her taste. I reach my hands to the bottom of her tee and draw it up and off. Her bra is next. This leaves her in skimpy shorts and panties. I move my hands back to her ass. God, it's perfect. I shove the elastic waist of her shorts down, taking the panties with them as I drop to my knees. She steps out of her shoes and kicks them aside. I slide my fingers along the crevice of her ass and smile when I hear her suck in air. My tongue follows my fingers as I lick a slick path down the seam of her ass cheeks.

"Fuck, I can't stand up," she moans.

I give her a hard shove and she falls face first on the bed. "Stay there," I tell her as I step two feet back and slam the door. "I'm going to fuck you just like that."

"Please tell me you have lube," she groans against the sheets while I divest myself of clothes. I have no lube but once we get started I think she'll forgive me.

I kneel down and separate her ass cheeks. They feel so damn good in my hands, and I massage her while I check out her dark hole. Not that I can really see anything but puckered skin. Fuck she's beautiful here. This morning my thumb told me how tight she is. I lean in and lick one ass cheek before sinking my teeth into her wicked flesh.

The groan that escapes her is half pain, half desire. "My naughty, naughty princess," I whisper as my tongue swirls across the teeth marks. Fuck I love her ass. I slip my finger lower to her pussy and slide through the wetness I knew was waiting for me. I glide my wet finger upward to her ass and circle it around the entrance. I add more of her silky heat before flicking my tongue over the hole.

She cries out and her fingers dig into the mattress.

I rise up and position myself above her and then sink into her pussy. She lets out a growl of frustration and I half groan, half laugh as I slowly slide in and out. She's tight and wet. I need wet. I strain to keep it slow until her pussy floods with silky lube. I pull out and move my dick to the only hole I'm interested in right now. I gather more wetness on my fingers and slide one in.

"God, oh God," she moans.

I work another finger in and her words become unclear. I slap my dick against her ass cheek as I slide my fingers in and out.

"Please, Dagger, please," she begs.

"My name is Dax. In this room, you'll use my name." I've waited to hear her say it and I can't think of a better time. I slide my hand beneath her pelvis and position her ass higher. With my other hand, I press the head of my cock against her. I don't bust down the door, I just slide in a bit and back out. She whimpers. "Take a breath, princess, and let me in," I command.

"I can't," she groans. "You need lube."

I growl my answer. "You have your own fucking lube, relax." I push a little more insistently.

"Fuck, Dagger."

I slap her ass. "Dax," I groan and push in a bit more.

"That," she wails.

That could only be slapping her ass. Works for me and I add a few more hard swats. She cries out and wiggles, which drives me crazy. I gain an inch. Keeping my hand beneath her, I slide the other over her hip and up her waist past her breasts. I circle her throat and add pressure. She tries to suck in air. It's then that her body gives into me and I slide my cock to the hilt.

"You fucking like that, princess, don't you?" She wheezes against my hand. I pull my cock out slowly while her muscles try to hold on. I know it's less painful for her if I don't pull out all the way, but my princess enjoys pain. I slide out of her ass and immediately push back in. This time she screams my name.

"Dax, fuck, Dax."

We play this game for as long as I can handle it. I use the hand I'm holding her hips up with and find her clit while adding pressure to her throat. She begins pulsing around my dick and I remove my hand from her neck. I slide it down and around and grab the back of her hair, pushing her face into the sheets. She can breathe somewhat and I'm not in danger of completely depriving her of oxygen when I lose control.

She lays still and quietly whimpers as I come inside her tight ass. Fuck, my orgasm goes on and on like I haven't come in weeks. I practically fall against her back when I can no longer hold myself up. She groans, so I roll us both to our sides so we face each other.

I move the hair from her face and find her lips. I can't get enough of this fucking woman. She's fucking perfect.

# 22

*Sofia*

**Dagger's such an asshole**.

He ordered me to clean the main room. I'm hot and sweaty and my muscles ache from moving tables and chairs with only Rufus' help. I've been here for six days and all I do is cook, clean, and fuck. I visit Red in the morning before it's too hot in the trailer. I have no idea how they stand it. Has anyone heard of air conditioners around here? The fucking thing they call an evap cooler does a piss poor job. At night it's too damn hot for Dagger to touch me after we've fucked. I'm barely sleeping and the asshole constantly seeks me out during the night like he's afraid I won't be there. I grumble and move away from his body heat. Then each day is the same. There's no TV and whoever has the iPod took it with them because there isn't any music either. I need fucking music to clean.

Poor Rufus takes the brunt of my bad mood and still manages to smile and whistle to some unknown beat in his head. I swept and mopped. The fucking guys will start spitting their chewing tobacco outside or I'll be poisoning their food. They're full-grown men and this disgusting habit is at an end. Rufus just shrugs when I go on my verbal tirade.

I'm making meatloaf for dinner and with it baking in the oven, the kitchen will be more sweltering than it is in the main room where I'm at now. There' a church meeting tonight and Dagger told me the officers would be at the club and that it's my job to feed them. I'm surprised steam isn't coming out my damned ears.

I hear the truck pull up out front but don't bother looking outside. I've decided not to speak to Dagger for a while. I'm shit at being the happy little Mexican who slaves for the white man. Fuck him.

Dagger opens the front door and grins at me when I look up. I ignore him. "Come see what I bought you, princess," he says cheerfully even with the snub.

No fucking way. I continue placing chairs at the tables. His heavy boots stomp across my clean floor and I'm about to come unglued when I'm hefted up and over his shoulder.

"You fucking prick," I yell.

"Come on, I know you're hot, so I bought you a gift."

He knows all right. I've done nothing but complain about the heat. Give me Florida humidity any day. I stop fighting him only because I'm worried I'll land on my ass. "Fine, put me down and I'll walk on my own," I huff. I'll also grab his knife and slit his throat if he gives me a chance.

"No way," he says as he carries me out the front door.

I arch my back so my face isn't against Dagger's ass. Skull removes a bandana from his head and wipes his brow. He's standing beside a box. A very large box. Dagger bends and my feet hit the ground. I squint up at him. He looks so damn proud of himself.

"You like it?" he asks with a grin.

"It's a big fucking box. What the hell is there to like? You know we sleep in these in Mexico, so I guess you could say you bought me a house," I say testily.

"Ha. Ha. Ha," he replies. "I bought the Latina princess an air conditioner and all she can do is bitch about it."

I look at the box. An air conditioner? I turn to Dagger and his grin widens. I throw myself at him and clench my legs around his waist as he staggers back. I rain kisses over his hot face and neck.

"I think the princess finally decided to lose the attitude, Skull. I may need to buy her an air conditioner every day."

Both men laugh. There are two more identical boxes in the back of the truck. "Three air conditioners?" I whisper against his neck.

"The ladies need one and we'll put one in the front room of the clubhouse too. The electric bills will eat us alive, so we'll only be using them to sleep and when we party. The kitchen will still be hot, but you'll need to wait on that one. There's not a good window to put it in and we'll need to cut a hole in the wall."

I swear I'm getting emotional over fucking air conditioners, but I truly want to cry. Dagger's smile melts my heart. He hefts me up a little higher, carries me around the side of the truck, and opens the door. There's a small bag inside lying on the bench seat, and he reaches in and grabs it. He raises the bag up toward my hands, which are still around his shoulders. I release my legs and slide down. I glance inside the plain white bag and see a box.

"It's nothing fancy, but you can use my laptop to download some music."

It's an MP3 player. I thought he wasn't paying attention to all the bitching I've been doing, but he's obviously heard every word. Damn, it must be close to my time of the month because tears well in my eyes. I wipe them away before they can fall. Dagger sees it and his face goes soft. "I like watching that sexy ass move," he says and pulls me back in close.

Our lips clash and I feel the kiss clear to my toes.

"While the two of you make out here in the hot sun, I'll just go inside and have a beer. Let me know when I can help install the bedroom air."

Dagger releases my mouth and smiles. "Only have time to install one unit today, princess. Your choice. Bedroom or club?"

It kills me. "Give the first one to the ladies. They need it more than I do."

Dagger's eyes shine and he kisses me again. I guess that was the right thing to say.

Skull interrupts the kiss. "When the officers get here they can help us install a unit so the trailer is cool and also the bedroom. We'll make it happen."

I feel exactly like the princess they call me.

# 23

*Dax*

**We hold church to** discuss the drug buy tomorrow. All of us are feeling antsy and I don't remember it being this intense before. We settle on the final plan and eat dinner in the big room.

Skull and I managed to install both units before the meeting began. The trailer was actually easy because the unit fit perfectly where the cooler was. The whores are able to enjoy dinner in a cool place while the rest of us suffer. Food is good, though, so I won't complain.

The brothers clear out early, and I fuck Sofia for more than an hour with the steady hum of the air conditioner keeping us cool. She's been pushing me away because of the heat, but tonight I fall asleep with her curled against my side.

The knock on the door wakes me a few hours later.

"Dagger," Red whispers. What the fuck? I slide the gun from under the mattress and uncoil myself from Sofia's arms. She doesn't stir. I slip on my jeans, move to the side of the door, and open it.

"I need to talk to you," Red whispers.

"What the fuck, Red?" I say as she slides through the door and closes it behind her.

"Red?" Sofia asks groggily.

I walk over and turn on the lamp squinting into the light. Red sits on the end of the bed.

"I wasn't exactly truthful about something I said the day you had me explain my side of the story about Sofia," she starts. My brain is having trouble figuring out what the hell she's talking about. "Why Fox kept me around," she clarifies.

"Okay," I say carefully.

"No one but Fox knew this and you can't tell the others. It's too dangerous."

"I'll determine that after you tell me what the fuck is going on," I snap.

"My brother. He's the Justice of the Peace for the county."

"What?"

"He signed a warrant a few hours ago to raid the club. He's been giving me a heads up for years and I tell Fox. That's why Fox needed me here. Judge Gunnler is actually my half-brother. He's as corrupt they come and Fox pays him for inside info when he comes through for us."

Fuck me. It makes sense. Fox kept the heat off our back and we all knew he had to have an inside. "When is the warrant going down?" I ask as I grab my phone.

"He wouldn't give them a night warrant, so it will be as soon as the sun comes up. I usually take all the drugs and hardware and slip out. My brother says they have eyes on us right now. I know there's paraphernalia, but we should be clear of drugs." She nods at my gun. "You'll go down for that too. I can carry a bag into the desert if I slip away in the next hour. They're hitting Skull and Vamp's places too."

"Fuck, you know what they have on us to gain a warrant?"

"Weapons and drugs. The affidavit says they got a tip from an anonymous informant. One of the deputies let it slip in front of my brother that it was a woman. My guess is Pauline."

"Fuck," I say again. "Okay, we'll start making calls. You'll need to take this phone with you too or the cops will confiscate it." I hand the phone to Sofia first. "Go through my list and quickly tell all the brothers what's going down," I tell her as I pull on my boots. "I'll start searching for paraphernalia." I look at Red. "Clear out whatever's in the trailer and meet me back here as soon as you can."

Red leaves as quickly as she arrived.

Sofia says Vampire's name into the phone and I'm glad she's notifying the guys on the crash-list first. I take the pillowcase off the pillow and put my gun inside. Most of the guys carry on their person, so there shouldn't be guns around the clubhouse. I found different drug shit when I cleaned this room. I stuck it in the bottom drawer of the dresser, so I grab it and cram it into the pillowcase. I head to the end of the hallway and knock on the door to the room Rufus took over. He sits up in bed and rubs his eyes when I turn on the light. I tell him in one clipped sentence what's happening. He jumps up, grabs his pants, and begins helping me.

Keeping the lights out, we clear the bar and check the other bedroom. We're worried that whoever's watching us will notice the lights and realize we know something's going down. We can't take a chance that they hit us right away even if the warrant won't be good. We find nothing more.

I take the phone from Sofia. She's calm and acts like this shit is a daily occurrence. Yep, my dick twitches. "Did you get everyone?"

"Yes, they're holding tight until they hear from you."

I send off a text and cancel the drug buy. Won't go over well, but we don't have a choice. My text is vague but gets my point across.

*Canceling appointment, legal issues.*

My next message goes to Gomez, Moon's enforcer.

*Mom talking, shit going down, I'll be in touch.*

Gomez's response is almost immediate.

*Need us?*

*We're good.*

The response about the drug buy comes in just as I'm about to add my phone to the pillowcase.

*You lost our business, we only dealt with Fox. Lose this number.*

Pauline must be talking to more than the cops. People say things about silver lining bullshit. This is ours and I'll take it. I don't reply, it's unnecessary. We are now officially out of the drug business. I toss my phone in the pillowcase along with Sofia's, which I slipped in my pocket from where I kept it in the dresser. Sofia's gun goes in too. Doesn't matter that it's hers. Never asked where she got it or if it's clean. She's under this roof, so my and Rufus' prison records will cause problems we don't need.

Red comes in with a handful of glass pipes and other assorted items we need to get rid of. Rufus' gun joins everything else and then Red takes off. She has a flashlight that she'll use when she's far enough away. She's stashing the pillowcase and heading back to the trailer to wait with the ladies.

I pull Sofia in close and hug her. "Sorry about this, princess. Stay dressed and try to get some sleep," I tell her.

"Are you sleeping?"

I look around the room and hope we caught everything. "I'll lie down with you."

It's four o'clock in the morning and neither of us sleep. I fucking hate this shit and my heart beats overtime until the sun peeks through the window and the front door crashes in.

Shouts of, "Sheriff's Department," come from the front and back of the building. I raise my hands when the bedroom door flies open. "Get on the floor, get on the floor. Keep your hands where we can see them."

Sofia cries out as she's jerked from the bed. I should have told her to immediately follow their instructions. I try to control my anger as she cries out again when they jerk her arms behind her back and snap cuffs on her. I'm shoved to my stomach and my face is pushed to the floor. *Fucking assholes.*

"What the hell did I do, shithead?" Sofia yells.

"Clear, clear," can be heard coming from all the rooms. One of the deputies roughly lifts me to my feet and walks me into the front room, where another deputy pushes me so I sit down against the wall by the front door. "We have a warrant," the deputy says. He could have told me to fucking sit down and I'd have complied. They like putting on their show and shoving everyone around. I hate these motherfuckers. Controlling my anger is near impossible, but I know from experience being angry will get me nowhere. Prison was like this every fucking day.

"No shit, really?" I spit out about the warrant. "Where's my woman? She hasn't done anything."

The deputy ignores my bitching. "Where's Frank Tison?" he demands.

"Frank who?" I play dumb even though I know damn good and well who he's talking about. This deputy is still wet behind the ears and doesn't appear smart enough to trick me into anything involving Fox's death. I'm thinking Pauline kept that info to herself for some reason.

Another deputy in full black riot gear steps forward. "Fox, where is he?"

This is the one I need to watch out for. He's special task force of some kind. "Cleared out a few days ago. Didn't like the changes," I say. Still no strange looks and I breathe a sigh of relief. I'm almost positive they don't know Fox is dead.

"Who's in charge?" he asks.

I'll lawyer up if they ask me anything I don't want to answer, but they'll know it's me soon enough. "I am. If you want me to answer more questions, get my woman out here so I can see she's okay."

He nods at the other deputy and the young one leaves the room.

"You got a name?" I ask.

"Agent Crier," he says, which answers my silent question. This guy is drug task force. They all have the distinction of "agent." Whatever gets their rocks off and all that.

"And your name?" he asks me.

"Dax Montgomery," I say.

Red and the other three ladies walk in through the door off the kitchen in handcuffs. They're followed by another deputy. Red's the only one who isn't crying. She's as pissed off as I am. I'm worried about Sofia. A minute later I hear her cussing as they walk her into the front room with the rest of us.

"You assholes. What the hell did I do? Worried a Latina woman will kick your ass so you need to restrain me?"

That right there shows that Sofia has never been in prison. She doesn't have the demeanor of someone who's ever needed to follow rules or face the consequences. I can't help my smile.

"No talking," says the deputy who brought in Sofia. Another deputy follows with Rufus.

"So I can't talk either? Who the fuck are you, God?" Sofia has her steely gaze directed fully on the deputy.

"They think they're God," Red adds to the mix.

"Everyone calm down," Agent Crier says. "Let us do our job and this will go quickly."

Now he receives the wrath of Sofia. "I was in bed thinking about blowin' my man and getting a lick or two of my own and you dog fuckers storm in and start throwing us around. This is bullshit."

I bite my lip praying he'll ask why she called him a dog fucker.

Agent Crier moves closer to Sofia. "And who are you?" he questions evenly.

"Name's Sofia Guadalupe Acosta. I'm here visiting and this is what I get? You assholes need a lesson in manners." Her hair's tangled and flying around as she jerks against the handcuffs. "These things are hurting my wrists, and I'll be taking pictures of the bruises."

"You need the cuffs loosened?" Crier asks as he reaches for the cuff key on his belt.

"Double lock them," I say when he leans down. Crier looks at me and nods. When you've spent time inside, you know the tricks. Double locking keeps the cuffs from going tighter as well as looser.

"Turn around," he tells Sofia.

She huffs out a breath but shuffles to her knees and turns. "I'm surprised to see someone like you visiting here. What's your story?" he asks while he fixes the cuffs.

*Don't fall for it*, I plead silently.

She shifts back around when the cuffs are adjusted and plops her ass on the floor. Her eyes are still spitting fire. "I have no fucking idea what you mean by *someone like me*," she says with scorn. "Came to spend some quality time with my dad. What's it to you?"

*Fuck!*

"Just making conversation. Who's your dad?"

*Fuck. Fuck!*

Sofia doesn't know when to shut up. "He goes by the name Fox. That's my daddy dearest," she says with fake sweetness.

Agent Crier's eyes snap back to mine. I was fucking wrong. They do know something's gone down with Fox. Crier knows exactly who I am, but he's playing dumb cop, which isn't a stretch for most of them. Crier's fucking smart, though, and I need to remember that. Of course Sofia might land my ass back in prison and everything I've tried to do will be for nothing.

Crier slowly turns back to her. "You seen your dad in the past few days?"

I'll personally take care of the bitch Pauline if I make it out of this. She fucking ratted everything, the sorry bitch.

"Daddy wasn't too keen on having a Latina baby girl and high-tailed it out when I hooked with my man there." She looks at me and her eyes go steamy. Hell, I'm falling for her theatrics and I know it's all bullshit.

"Where did he go?" Crier demands in a louder voice. This obviously wasn't what he expected.

"Took off and said fuck the club. I've been cooking and providing extra services for my man. We want a whole passel of little bald babies with dark skin. These boys have decided to get with the times and integrate. I've invited a few of my chicas from back home. The boys here will pay us to cook and clean. Fucking's optional, which is a pretty good deal for the likes of us."

I've never heard her lay on the Spanish accent so thick or the dumb Latina routine. I lean my head back against the wall and look up at the ceiling while she continues talking.

"Dax, my man, is turning this club around. No drugs and no breaking the law. Daddy dearest didn't like that he was outvoted. This here is a democratic club now. The ladies you have in cuffs are clean for the first time in years. You can just think of this place as rehab for druggies and reformed bigots."

The look on Crier's face is priceless. Sofia is so enthusiastic it's hard not to believe her. Rufus snickers softly beside me and Crier turns to us. His light brown eyes are darker now and I'm guessing he isn't happy.

"She's right. Club's turning over a new leaf. We're all about diversity now," I add with as much sugar in my voice as I can manage.

Crier shakes his head and walks away stopping at another guy dressed in riot gear. The two of them speak quietly. It sucks that I can't hear what they're saying. Additional deputies enter and under Crier and his buddy's direction begin tearing the place apart.

"I hope you wiped your boots off. I mopped those floors yesterday," Sofia taunts.

I just shake my head, sit back, and enjoy the show. I watch Crier and his bud's frustration climb the longer the guys search without finding anything. They carry my laptop out, which is clean, but it will be in their hands for months. I need it to work on plans for the convenience store, so I'm not happy. Crier walks back over an hour later.

His pleasant expression is back. "You mind if we search your car parked in the back?" he asks Sofia.

"You got a warrant?" she quips.

"No," he crouches down to her level. "We didn't see the car before we got the warrant signed."

She smiles and bats her pretty brown eyes. "Too fucking bad. No, you can't search my car. I keep my extra sex toys in the trunk and I don't want your dirty hands on them. They cost a lot of money and I've been collecting those babies for years. If my old man's away," she nods toward me, "I need something to help flick the bean. I'm a girl with high needs."

Crier doesn't bother responding to her jibes; he just stands and walks away. I can no longer contain my grin. An hour later, we're uncuffed and Crier hands me a receipt for what they confiscated along with the copy of the warrant. I had a clean, throwaway phone that I intentionally left for them to find. He's unhappy but does his best not to show it.

"You really trying to clean this club up?" he asks me.

"It's done," I tell him.

He gives me a chin lift and leaves. We stand at the window and watch the ten plus cars clear out. When the dust settles, I turn to Sofia, pick her up, and twirl her around.

She laughs until I stop and pull her in for a deep kiss.

# 24

*Sofia*

**The cops destroyed the** place. It takes us more than an hour to get everything back in order. Brothers start showing up and Rufus runs his mouth repeatedly. I'm a pretty hot topic right now. I guess my job was to play the nice, quiet Latina while the white man fucked me over. They don't know me well because I'll never be intimidated by those assholes. I haven't done anything and the secrets I hold are between me and God.

I was pissed off about Dagger's wrist and that they handcuffed him. He doesn't wear the brace to bed, but I've seen him massaging it since the cuffs came off. He hasn't put the brace back on and the last thing I'll do is whine at him for it.

Some of the guys who weren't too fond of keeping me around are now giving me chin lifts. I've concluded that men have an entire chin language that females are ignorant of. I give my own lift back, but it just doesn't work for me like it does for them.

The cops even attacked the refrigerator. At least they threw everything back inside so it didn't spoil. Dagger enters the kitchen just as I'm rearranging the last items. His hands go to my hips and he pulls my ass against his hard dick. I wiggle for his benefit. I'm still pissed off about what those assholes did to the clubhouse. It isn't much, but I've worked my butt off cleaning this place and they didn't give a shit.

"Brothers want to barbeque tonight," he whispers in my ear and then proceeds to bite my earlobe.

I'm getting past my anger real quick and my heart rate picks up. I wiggle my ass again and Dagger's hands skim along my waist until he cups both breasts. "Fuck, Sofia, you fucking handled the cops and turned me the fuck on while doing it. I've never had a hard-on during a search warrant."

I raise my arms and circle his neck while leaning my head back against his shoulder. He looks down at me and scratches his unshaven chin against my neck and cheek. "We're letting the cold out of the refrigerator," I say huskily.

He moves us away from the door and shuts it before turning me around. His hands are back at my hips and he lifts me to the kitchen counter. Hell, his eyes burn. I'm sure mine are the same way. He stands between my thighs, runs one hand through my hair, and brings a section to his nose. He inhales and closes his eyes. It's so damn sexy. His head has tufts of hair now that's just becoming noticeable. I rub one hand across the bristly texture.

"I'm letting it grow," he says.

"I like," I murmur back.

"What else do you like?" he asks while nuzzling my neck. "Flicking the bean I think is what you called it. You want me flicking your bean?"

I laugh. "That's exactly what I want."

I groan when Dagger releases me and steps back. He pulls my shorts and panties off with a little assistance from me as I lift my ass at the appropriate time.

"Tongue or cock?" he asks with a sensual smile that leaves my pussy dripping. What a choice.

"Tongue tonight, cock now." I unbuckle his belt and help him push his jeans over his hips. He lifts me from the counter and slides me over his cock. I circle his neck with my hands and his hips with my legs. He bites my shoulder where the skimpy tank reveals skin.

"In the kitchen?"

I glance up and see Vampire standing in the doorway.

"Get the fuck out," Dagger groans.

"Ya don't need to tell me again, brother. Your white ass lights up the entire room. I'll keep the brothers out so you can enjoy your taco in private."

"Oh, God." I bury my face in Dagger's shoulder.

"I'll kick his ass when we're done."

"Why?" I ask on a sigh as Dagger thrusts his cock deep.

"For referring to you as a taco," he says quietly.

Our strained breathing fills the room as he continues sliding in and out. "He's referring to my pussy. Heard it before. I'll kick his ass myself when it's needed."

Dagger groans loudly. "You done talking?"

"Fuck me harder and I'll shut up." I rub my breasts against his chest wishing we were skin to skin.

"It's the best taco I've ever had," he whispers and it's the last understandable words spoken.

Dagger holds church to talk about the warrant. It's beginning to get to me that I don't know what's being said in that damn room. Red assures me we find out sooner or later. She's helping me prepare for the barbeque.

"The ladies are coming tonight," I tell her.

She stops slicing tomatoes knowing exactly what I'm saying. "It'll get pretty rowdy if they're here and some of the guys bring old ladies."

"So?" I say.

"The guys fuck the whores when the old ladies aren't around. The two groups don't mix."

I stop shredding lettuce and give my full attention to Red. "The guys with old ladies fuck the whores?" I ask baffled.

"When the old ladies aren't around, which with Fox was most of the time."

"That's fucked up. Those bald twats screw around on their old ladies?"

"It's the way it is, Sofia."

"Not anymore. You let the ladies know if they put their hands on my man, I'll break their fingers. Unattached men only or their puta asses will feel my boot."

Red's laugh is long and loud. "You better discuss this with Dagger. The brothers won't be happy."

"If the brothers are fucking around on their old ladies, they shouldn't *be* fucking happy. I won't hold with that shit and I'd hate to cut someone's balls off."

Her laughter gets louder. I don't find it funny at all.

Everyone shows up to grill. Rufus and some of the other guys carried tables and chairs outside. They strung up a giant canopy, but the sun still hits most of the tables.

"They won't start cooking until the sun is setting," Charlie tells me. She's in high spirits and not upset at all that the police served a search warrant on her house this morning. "Keeps us on our toes," is all she says about it.

AJ's old lady, Samantha, has a bun in the oven and she doesn't handle the heat too well. She's just starting to show, which is cute. AJ is one of the men who never really looked at me with respect until today. He dotes on his wife and gives the evil eye to the guys who get out of hand with the jokes. She's blonde and beautiful in a white trash kind of way. Her breasts overflow her top and I'm not sure if it's the pending kid or if she's naturally gifted. We'll see how firm those titties are after she gives birth and has a baby sucking on them.

She's shy and doesn't say a lot to me. I don't get the vibe that it's a white versus Latina thing. Her fair skin shows a constant blush even without the rowdy talk. Loki, one of the brothers, keeps his arms around Tramp. She's one of the women coming off drugs. She doesn't seem to mind Loki hanging on her, but I plan to watch the two of them. These women no longer need to whore for drugs. They have a choice. Dagger will have blue balls if he says anything differently. Red is happy and hangs on Curly. He grabs her boobs and plants her on his lap every chance he gets.

It's hotter than hell and I escape inside every ten minutes to cool down. The guys hooked up the air conditioner for the front room earlier, so it's semi-cool inside. I stand in front of the vents until I'm cooler. Then it's off to the kitchen to carry out more food.

I turn from the counter when I hear the kitchen door open. Bear walks in and places his hands up when I give him a *what the hell* look. I don't entirely trust him even though his attitude has improved greatly. "Thought I'd help you carry some of this out if you want my help."

"You got something to say?" I ask because I don't believe him.

"Yeah," he answers while giving me a hard stare. "You saved our ass. Yeah, you can cook and clean, but that didn't mean we could trust you. Now we can. You need help, I'm your man."

"I have a man," I tell him completely misunderstanding.

He grins. "You're one of us. Not a brother but still one of us. We have your back."

I'm no good with this shit. "You've made your point. Yes, I need help if your wimpy arms can handle it."

"You're gonna give Dagger a run for his money. You'll make a strong old lady for our prez. We need that. Your man has some good ideas and it's more than most of us have ever had."

This is getting soppy and I can't even look at him. I carry my tray out and he follows with another one. Do I want to be an old lady? Is it something you need to be asked, like marriage? I don't understand these rules. AJ and Samantha are married. Skull and Charlie are married. I don't know about the rest. Well... Red isn't married to Curly, so that makes me feel better. Fucking a guy and marriage are two different things. Whereas, I was warm a few minutes ago, I feel clammy now. I'm not a settle-down type of woman. I don't think anyone would stop me if I decide to leave now. I want a little more time with Dagger before I move on. It feels nice that I'm no longer held here. It gives me the freedom to enjoy this time while fucking Dagger's brains out. My goal is to make sure he never forgets my Latina ass. I disregard the ache in my chest when I think about leaving. *Buck up chica*, I tell myself.

On one of my next trips inside, Samantha is in the kitchen. "You have my permission to cut off AJ's balls if he's with one of the whores," she says straight up. She isn't nearly as shy as I gave her credit for, and I guess Red's been blabbing her mouth.

"You better warn him first so he knows what's coming if he crosses the line."

"I can do that," she says with a smile.

How can I not smile back at this blonde Barbie. I wonder if she'll wear five-inch heels when her belly's the size of a basketball. Wouldn't surprise me if she can. She carries a bag of ice out while I handle two. We dump them into a large tin tub that has beer, soda, and water. The sun is setting, but it isn't any cooler.

Dagger walks up and slings his arm across my shoulder. "You hungry?"

He's shirtless with sweat coursing down his chest. He's wearing his signature bandana around his brow. How can a white guy grow on me this quickly? His arm is hot where it touches my skin.

"Starving," I reply.

He laughs in his low sexy way. "I think you're always hungry for that. I meant real food and not just snacks," he teases.

"Yeah, food too."

His lips are warm. He deepens the kiss and a few whistles go out from the guys. Dagger ignores them and takes his time. Fuck. What if he thinks I'm his old lady? I push back and twist away from him. "I have more to bring out if you're getting the grill started."

He appears surprised and gives me a long look before shrugging and turning to the guys. "Who's playing chef tonight?"

I escape to the kitchen.

Maybe I should leave sooner rather than later.

# 25

*Dax*

**It's been three weeks** since the warrant. Sofia runs hot and cold and I have no idea what the hell her problem is. She has issues that far exceed my issues and I don't know what to do.

She works the club like it's her lot in life, but I can tell she doesn't enjoy cooking and cleaning so much. I told her a few days ago to ease off and she didn't speak to me for the rest of the day. She wraps anger around her like a shield.

It's also hard to get any real privacy in this place because someone is always underfoot and the walls are paper thin. After dinner and while the guys are partying, I'm bringing her back to this room until we settle whatever the fuck is going on.

She went all out and served lasagna with bread sticks tonight. They melt in my mouth. The guys love her for her cooking alone. She told me a few weeks ago that she worked off and on in different restaurants. She clammed up when I started prying deeper. The woman has more secrets than anyone I've ever known.

"Come on," I tell her when we're finished eating. I take her hand and lead her behind me toward the bedroom.

"I need to clean the kitchen. Your dick can wait until I'm finished," she snaps.

"I handled that. Whores are cleaning up tonight." She hates when I call them whores, so I did it on purpose. She has a short fuse, but she's been allowing it to die out as fast as it comes on. Even I know this isn't like her. I want my fiery Latina back. Tonight I want answers and I plan to use her quick temper against her until I know what the fuck is going on.

We slip into the room and I close the door behind us. Her hands go to her hips. "I can clean the kitchen myself," she challenges.

"I'm aware of that. You can clean the club, do the laundry, shop, and cook too. Good for you. It must be that subservient Latina blood of yours."

Her head immediately lifts higher. "What the fuck did you just say?"

"You heard me. Now be the good little Latina and lose the clothes and get on your back."

I expect her fists flying at my face but not the knee she tries to de-man me with. Luckily she connects with my thigh. "Need to work on that move, princess." I've captured her right fist in my hand and I'm ready for the other one. I also pull her in close so her legs aren't as big a threat.

Her body goes lax, but she doesn't fool me. "What the fuck are you doing, Dagger?" she huffs out and flicks her head so her hair goes over her shoulder.

"I'm tired of your attitude and everything you're doing to avoid me except when we hit the bed at night."

"What? You act like I'm your old lady or something."

Hmm. Is that what this is about? "Do you need a formal invitation to be my old lady, princess?"

Something strange flashes in her eyes. "Fuck you, the last thing I want is to be some skinhead's old lady."

And we're back to this. "You fuck like you want it."

"You prick," she screams.

I'm surprised at the violence of the sound, and I release her. She stumbles back a foot.

"Sofia, what the hell is up?" I ask in clear confusion. She wipes her hand at the corner of her eye. Tears? What the fuck is happening?

"It's time for me to move on. I have a life I want to get started now that I don't need to spend every waking minute thinking about killing Fox. You need to let me go, Dagger."

She's serious.

"I'm not letting you go, Sofia, so put that thought right out of your fucking head," I say in desperation and without really thinking about exactly what the words might mean to her.

"So, I'm still your prisoner after everything I've done? I'm not good enough to just walk away?"

I'm fucking this up royally. "No, that's not what I meant."

"You think I don't know exactly what you mean?" she grinds out. Her hands start fisting in and out. "My mother was Fox's possession and his punching bag. From what I've seen in life that's what the kind of relationship you and I have is all about. I won't take that shit, so it's better if I leave now because I will kill your ass if you ever hit me."

Fuck. I run my hand across my head. "If you're talking about the day you came to the club, which is the only time I've hit you, I didn't have much choice, but I sure as fuck wasn't proud of it."

"That's what you say now. I have a temper and I use my fists to keep people in line. It's not exclusively a man's trait."

"So why the fuck have you pulled back from confrontation? Where's that hot temper you're so proud of?" She looks stricken, but I go on. "You want to use your fists on me, go ahead. I'll be damned if I ever hit you back, but if that's your thing, take your best shot." Her palm comes out and plants solidly in my chest causing me to move back an inch. "That it?" I taunt.

Her other fist takes me in the face. My head turns with the blow and my lip splits. I wipe the blood away. "What the fuck are you doing, Sofia?"

Her eyes are wild and I have no idea what's going on in her fucked up head. "Hit me back, damn you," she says in desperation.

I catch her raised fist before she hits me again. "No. I just said I would never hit you."

"You know you fucking want to," she screams and jerks her fist from my hand.

"No, I don't."

She backs up another six inches, which makes her feet a bigger threat than her fists. I get ready to block another attempt at my balls. Before I can stop her, she throws the door open and runs from the room. I'm on her heels as she heads to the front room.

It's obvious the guys were listening because they're all looking at the two of us like we've lost our minds. I think one of us has. Sofia doesn't stop until she's in front of Bear, who is unfortunate enough to be standing. He's not prepared when she drives her fist into his nose. I think the entire room hears the crunch. Fuck. How the hell did this get so out of hand?

"Go ahead, hit me, Bear. Hit the fucking Latina like you want to."

Blood floods out of Bear's nose and between the fingers that are now holding his face. His eyes are watering. Somehow he keeps half his attention on Sofia while looking at me in utter confusion. I grab her from behind and her legs kick out. She turns into the wildcat from the first day.

The brothers are struggling with the same shock I am.

"Let her go, Dagger," Skull says. "Let her get it out."

He's the only person I've mentioned her mood to. He's crazy if he thinks she'll stop now. I release her anyway. I haven't the foggiest clue what to do.

She immediately turns and faces me. "You think I haven't been hit plenty of times in my life that I can't take it?"

"No, princess, that's not what I think."

She spins around and faces the guys. "Go ahead, who wants the first shot?" She strikes her fists above her breasts. "Hit me, go ahead."

"No one's gonna hit you, Sofia. No one wants to." I want to cry, though. Me the big bad biker is swamped by emotion due to this woman who doesn't see what's right in front of her—love, respect, and family.

"Yes, they do," she shouts. "They all want to. Every man I've known in my whole damned life wanted to. Foster parents, they fucking have no problem with it. My mom's dealer. He always had a quick hand. Someone fucking hit me," she screams again.

"Princess, no one here will ever hit you. You want to break another nose, go ahead if it will make you feel better."

She half turns while watching the guys. Her breath is coming in and out from her lungs in loud pants. Her hands drop to her sides. When she faces me, her eyes are wide and her expression is nothing I can describe. Tears well over and roll down her cheeks.

"I'm fucking crazy, Dagger. No one in my entire fucking life has been able to handle me. You don't want the fucked up mess I am. Everyone will want me gone and I'll be thrown out like a piece of trash." Her head is shaking wildly.

Ah, hell. I step closer, afraid she'll run or worse start fighting again. I pull her in against my chest. Her hands lift and her fingernails dig into my chest between us. Her huge sobs are muffled by my shirt. I look at Skull over her head. Then I look at all the men. We're a fucking club of rejects. Each of us with nightmares we don't talk about. And I don't think any of us feel those nightmares are any worse than Sofia's. What she doesn't understand is that, for better or worse, she's one of us.

"I'm sorry, princess," I say into her hair.

"God, Dagger, fuck. I don't know what I'm doing. I expected to die when I came here. I should have died."

"No, baby, don't say that. You aren't trash. We need you. This entire club has your back and not a man here will ever let anyone lay a hand on you. You have my promise."

Skull approaches and places his hand on her back. "My promise too, Sofia."

One by one, each man walks over and assures her that she's one of us. When Rufus steps forward, he wipes his eyes. "My only job is to keep you safe. I'll do it forever. Don't you worry now."

She won't turn and face the men and that's okay. I lift and cradle her against my chest as I carry her back to our room. She curls into my arms on the bed with all her clothes on while I whisper assurances and run my fingers through her hair.

"No one has ever wanted me. I'm so afraid, Dagger, afraid you and the brothers will get rid of me," she cries softly.

"You're stuck being my old lady," is the last thing I say before her breathing slows and I know she's asleep.

I love her, and all I can do is pray she doesn't leave. Because if she tries, I won't stop her.

# 26

*Dax*

**It's been two weeks** since Sofia's meltdown. That's what she jokingly calls it. I watch her carefully and I'm glad to see her dark mood that led up to what happened is gone for now. She's happy. The real change has been in her not holding back her feelings when something pisses her off. She's my feisty hot Latina again with strong emotions. The guys can handle it and the rest of us enjoy watching when one of us is singled out and she goes off. She's using her voice and keeping her fists to herself.

"I've always been a throwaway. I was just waiting for it to happen again," she told me the morning after the meltdown.

Those words broke my heart.

When she apologized to Bear, he pulled her in for a crushing hug. She baked him a cake that night and told him he didn't need to share. He did of course.

The whores are back working the bar and front room. Sofia's message regarding cheating on old ladies made an impact. The attached men keep their hands to themselves. No one wants to face the wrath of Sofia, as it's now known. If she says she'll cut off their dicks, they don't doubt it.

I'm proud to have her as an old lady. The entire club is proud of her. She still cooks and we're all thankful. Red's ladies do the majority of the cleaning under Sofia's direction too.

The club is riding steady and we've been waiting for the permits to come through so we can put our business plans into action. It's with a sense of satisfaction that I stare at the envelope from the county. I submitted all the paperwork for the store weeks ago and this is the go-ahead we need. I tear into the envelope and start reading. Sofia walks up and peers over my shoulder.

"They've turned you down?" she whispers.

She's reading faster than I am. My eyes skim the words and my heart sinks. "Fuck."

"It says the County Board of Supervisors disapproved your proposal. How can they do that?"

I know the how and why. We're a fucking club of ex-cons. Each of us with a felony record. I was fucking stupid to think they would give us a shot. Hell, everything was riding on this. We could open a motorcycle shop here on the property but we'd get little business. We need to be on the highway.

"Dagger." Sofia places her hand on my back.

I shrug her hand off. "I need to ride," I say and place the paperwork on the closest table and walk out. I head to my bike and start her up. I take off after putting on the shades I keep in my saddlebag. Sofia didn't follow me and I know she'll be pissed off when I come back, but I need space.

Fuck.

I hit the highway and pick up speed. An hour later I'm in Phoenix on the 101 Loop. Twenty minutes later, I pull in front of the large iron gates that surround Moon's home. Two very large guards walk out to greet me. I turn off the engine and climb off my bike.

"Are Moon or Gomez available? They don't know I'm here."

"Moon knows you're here," one guy says. I think his name is Rack. He's one of the guys who tied me to the rafter in the garage before Gomez began beating the shit out of me.

"Let him in," Gomez says from behind the gate. "Bring your bike inside," he adds.

The men don't question Moon's enforcer, and a minute later, I'm rolling my bike in front of the monstrosity of a house. Gomez shakes my hand when I hop off the bike. He's in a suit and tie that reeks power. I look like shit in my dusty jeans and dirty T-shirt. He doesn't blink an eye. On closer inspection, I can see he's tired. Exhausted is more like it.

"How are you, Dax? The wrist looks good."

I hold up my wrist and fist my hand without pain. His goons broke it when they pulled a car maneuver and caused me to wreck my bike. "Better than the bike. Haven't had time to get the thing fixed properly yet. She needs bodywork and a paint job. How are you?" His massive shoulders shrug, which is so out of character for him. "How's Kiley and Celina?" I ask more pointedly.

"They're good. We got them out of state. Safer that way. Thanks for the heads up with the warrant. We felt no backlash, so everything must be clear on your end."

This man had the hots big time for Celina, Kiley's aunt. I'm surprised he allowed her out of his sight. Could be the cause for his sleepless nights. "They found nothing and left with their tails between their legs. Doesn't mean they won't be back."

"Come on inside and we'll talk where it's cool." He turns and I follow. I've been inside the house before. It's more of a museum. Moon lives here with his wife, Madison. I met her the same night I met Gomez, Moon, and Celina. I'm led to the room we had our meeting in before. "Moon's on his way in. You want something to drink?"

"I'll take water if it isn't a problem."

Gomez shakes his head and says, "No problem." He picks up the phone on the side table and pushes a button. "Do you mind bringing us two waters, Gabriella?"

He listens for a moment. "Gracias," he replies and puts the receiver down. "Take a seat. I'm guessing this is business not pleasure. If I'm wrong, we can head out to the pool. The misters and umbrellas keep it fairly nice."

I can't imagine sitting outside in a full suit. I have no idea how he stays cool in that thing. "In here works." I run my hand over my head. "I don't really know why the fuck I'm here. I owe you a debt and the club will pay it—"

Moon enters while I'm talking and he interrupts. "I think it's the other way around," he says. I stand up and shake his outstretched hand. Madison—she prefers to be called Mak—follows and ignores my hand and pulls me in for a hug. Moon's lips curl slightly, which is about as close to a smile as he gives. An older Spanish woman walks in and rests four bottles of water on the table before turning on her heels and walking out. Before we can settle at the table the woman is back carrying a tray filled half with vegetables and half with small sandwiches. She snaps something in Spanish at Gomez and he rolls his eyes.

"She's telling him he's too skinny and needs to eat," Mak says conspiratorially. "He's not handling Celina's absence well and we're all tired of his moping around and the way his suits hang on him."

"Does she ever stop?" Gomez grumbles at Moon.

"No, I don't believe she does." Moon replies with a soft look in Mak's direction.

Moon is also dressed in a suit and tie. Mak wears a classy skirt and blouse with flat sandals that manage to show off her legs. I have trouble reconciling her past as a cop and the fact she now runs Moon's escort service. She proves it takes a tough woman to handle the head of Arizona and New Mexico's largest crime syndicate. Her casual demeanor shows that Moon and Gomez don't intimidate her in the least.

Her eyes turn to me. "Please tell me you've found a good woman to keep you in line?" she asks.

Of all the things to affect me. Heat rises in my face.

Mak misses nothing. "Really, do tell. Who is she?"

Moon takes her hand and gently squeezes her fingers. "I believe this is a business meeting, baby."

"Haven't you heard of small talk to set the mood?" She turns her attention back to me. She's like a dog in search of the bone he hid a week ago. "So, who is she?"

"Fox's daughter," I reply honestly.

Her eyes go round. "Shit, you're kidding me."

"I should add—his Hispanic, or Latina as she prefers, daughter. She planned to kill Fox and when I took care of the problem before she could, she paid me back by aiming a gun at me and pulling the trigger."

Madison laughs. "That's priceless. We're glad she's a bad shot."

I shake my head. "No. She pulled the shot. I have a feeling there's nothing she can't do. She's nothing like her father. Rough life, traveled here from Florida. She heard about Kiley through one of the club ladies and decided she had to do something about it. Didn't know that Kiley was in good hands. She wasn't too happy that I took out her old man. She wanted that particular pleasure herself."

"You must bring her here. I already love her," Mak says.

I give a slight grin. "I think she'd like you too."

"Business," Gomez says testily. Yep, he's not doing well with Celina out of the picture. I won't ask if this is a permanent situation, but I'm thinking it is or he wouldn't be so bad-tempered.

"Look, I'm not here for help and I'm sorry, Moon, but the Desert Crows owe you. All the brothers agree and we pay our debts. What I need is advice." I look around the room and outline everything that's happened up until I rode away this afternoon. I have no idea if they have another *legal* direction I can take the club or not. I hope so. I really need to take an alternative back to the brothers.

It's after eleven when I'm on my bike again and heading home. Of course Moon wanted to help and not just offer advice. My pride kept me from taking him up on the offer. They are handling Pauline, though. Not killing her but making her disappear. It's what's best for Celina and Kiley, so I agreed to let them handle it. Mak made it clear that they wouldn't kill her. I'm not as generous, so I've turned it over to Moon's organization. Moon and Gomez didn't seem happy about keeping Pauline alive, but Moon will do what it takes to keep his woman off his back.

I have no idea if Sofia will be awake when I arrive at the club. One thing I do know—I'll have a pissed off Latina on my hands. I ride practically the entire way with a hard dick.

# 27

*Sofia*

I have no idea what's happening, and no one has heard from Dagger. Skull and Charlie showed up for a short time. Skull read the paperwork from the county and offered an explanation to why their permits were turned down.

"Some asshole, most likely the agent who handled the search warrant, mouthed off to the county board," he said. "We all have criminal records. No way we'll get those permits now."

I'm pissed off and have been since Dagger stormed out.

"Dagger will be back when he's cooled down," Skull told me before leaving. "He needed a ride to get his head on straight."

It hurts that Dagger didn't at least take me with him. Fuck, I'm his old lady and he should have me there when things are going good *and* bad. I refuse to allow my personal doubts to cloud my mind for long, so I spend two hours on the computer reading articles and blogs about ex-felons. The county is idiotic. The recidivism when felons find good jobs or start businesses is really low compared to the ones who don't.

Dagger is doing everything he can to take the Crows out of illegal activity. He told the damn agent that. They've done their time and deserve another chance.

A plan to help with this mess develops and I print off all the forms needed for the county. I have no idea if Dagger will go for it, but it's worth a try. I head to bed at midnight and a short time later I hear Dagger. I breathe a sigh of relief. Doesn't matter what Skull said, I was worried.

I listen to him undress and then he slides in behind me and pulls me against his naked body. I'm in a nightshirt and panties. Dagger's warm hand slides over my hip beneath the shirt.

"I'm sorry, princess."

My anger floats away as he dips lower and sneaks under my panties. "I was worried," I say breathlessly.

"I know," he whispers. "I needed to ride."

He moves my leg up so he can slip a finger inside me. I moan at the contact. "I want tongue," I whisper and he knows exactly what I'm talking about. He moves down the bed and takes my panties with him. I pull my shirt over my head and bend my knees when he's between my legs. He reaches over and turns on the light. I'm not surprised. Dagger is a very visual man. I keep my eyes closed, cover my breasts with my hands, and start to play with my nipples.

"That's right, princess, pinch those babies."

I pinch as he slides his tongue along my pussy lips. Fuck, it feels wonderful. His hands move beneath my ass and he lifts me solidly against his amazing mouth. This isn't just a treat for me; Dagger eats a woman like it's his last meal. God, his mouth, lips, and tongue are incredible. "Dax," I say quietly.

"Yes, princess, I've got you and I'm not letting go until you scream my name."

He finds my clit and sucks it past his lips. I no longer need to ask—one large finger slides into my ass and I moan loudly. He chuckles and gets back to work. His tongue is unbelievable as he swirls it around my entrance before sucking my clit again. I'm riding the waves when he slides another finger in my ass. It hurts and I whimper. He doesn't stop. He knows I want more. I'm pushing my feet against the mattress and grinding up against his mouth. Oh, God, he uses his teeth and nibbles on my clit. It hurts, my ass hurts. He slides his fingers in and out. It's too much and before I want it to end, I fly over the top screaming his name loud enough for Rufus to hear me from the other room. It won't be the first time, nor the last.

Dagger moves from between my legs and rises up above me. His hair is almost an inch long now. He looks like a completely different man. His cock rams inside my quivering pussy setting off a mini orgasm. He lifts my right leg and puts it over his shoulder as he moves into another position. Dagger loves to watch my pussy as his cock slides in and out. I reach my hands behind me and press them to the wall. He'll torment both of us with slow leisurely strokes until I come undone again.

I love him.

Nothing good ever lasts in my life. My eyes slide open and I see that he's looking at me. He smiles and my panic recedes. "You're so beautiful, princess," he says and looks back down where our bodies join.

I close my eyes and ride out the next wave. He's still going when it tapers off. He pulls out and flips me over. He jerks my hips up and drives in deep. Slow is over. Dagger fucks me hard and his groans fill the room. I'm crying his name over and over, when his cock begins pulsing inside me. My hands are filled with the pillow. He pulls out and slaps my ass, making me laugh.

He rolls me so I'm looking up at him. "Ah, dirty girl, I'll never get enough of you."

"Flip the light off and let me sleep," I whisper in exhaustion. "I'll show you a dirtier girl in the morning."

"Dirty pussy, my favorite." He turns out the light and pulls me in close.

I love this man so damn much.

# 28

*Dax*

**We're at the table** and I've allowed Sofia here to talk to the officers and present her plan. It could actually work. She filled out the paperwork last night while I was cooling my heels in the wind.

"You lease me the property and I apply for the permits. I'm Latina—a minority and female. I don't have a criminal record. I can scream from here to next year if they refuse me those permits. Do you really give a fuck if my name is on the paperwork?"

She lays the papers out on the table.

"You think they'll give you the permits just because you're Latina?" AJ asks.

I bite my lip and let Sofia handle this.

"Don't get your white boy panties in a wad. There aren't many perks for having brown skin. This just so happens to be one of them. The government thinks Latinas are good at things besides cooking, cleaning, and fucking."

AJ raises his hands in surrender. "Not what I meant, but do you mind if I comment that you're damn good at two of those?"

"All three," I mutter and receive a glare from Sofia.

AJ laughs and picks up one of the papers. "I say we go for it. Couldn't fucking hurt to give it a try at this point."

"I'm in," Skull adds.

Vampire agrees too.

Johns speaks up. "We can lease the property to her for a dollar a month to make it legit. Hell, we can pay her ten years or more in advance."

"How do you think the brothers will feel about me having my name on the papers?" Sofia asks and looks around the table.

Skull interlaces his fingers and pops his knuckles. "They'll like it because I tell them to like it." He's serious. Not only does Sofia have Bear protecting her, Skull has made it his personal project that none of the brothers gives her so much as a side eye.

"I say we vote," I tell the board.

Yeahs go up around the table. It's unanimous.

Sofia smiles. "I'll head over this afternoon. I need to take my car. Is there a problem if I go alone? I think it will look better in case there are eyes in the office that might know what we're about."

I give her a smile. "Sounds good. Is there gas in that thing?" It hasn't moved since the day she arrived.

"Enough to get me to Globe. I'll fill up there." She stands and moves closer to me, ignoring the men in the room. She leans in and kisses me. It's short and sweet. I'm not going for it. I pull her back when she tries to move away.

"This is why we keep pussy out of church. Too distracting," AJ grumbles.

I don't give a fuck. He's jealous he doesn't have his own woman in here. I finally release her when the complaining from all of them grows too loud. Sofia is flushed and my dick is semi-hard. If there was time and we didn't have more to discuss, I would cut out and take her to our room.

I quickly sign the lease paperwork and Skull co-signs. I surprise Sofia by handing her the keys to her car. I knew how the vote would go and I also knew I needed to trust her to do this alone. She smiles and gives me another quick kiss before leaving the room.

"Hell, that woman has you wrapped around her finger."

"More like she has her fingers wrapped around my cock and I want to keep it that way," I throw back.

They laugh and we continue the meeting.

# 29

*Sofia*

**Freedom. They trust me** enough to allow me to drive out alone. Until now, Rufus or Dagger has been with me every second. I've tried not to let it bother me but it has.

The papers are beside me on the passenger seat. I crank up the rock music. I can listen to about everything *but* country. I sing along with Aerosmith while tapping my fingers against the steering wheel. I take the turnoff for Globe, happy that my air conditioner works in this heat. They tell me the humid season hasn't begun yet and that's when it's really miserable. I've lived in Florida since I was a baby. I like the heat to a point. Now that we have air conditioning and it's bearable inside the clubhouse, I'm enjoying the desert more.

Saguaros pepper the hills. Dagger told me they're the state tree. Six to eight foot cacti is what they look like to me. Trees offer shade and have leaves. I'll admit these do offer a majestic beauty that I'm starting to appreciate.

This stretch of highway is pretty much deserted. I see the flash of a vehicle far behind me and keep singing to tunes as the desert flies by. From my rearview mirror, I notice the vehicle gaining on me. When it's a few hundred yards back, I realize the vehicle is actually two motorcycles.

"Fucking Dagger," I say aloud. He should have just said he didn't trust me to take this trip alone. I haven't had a burst of temper this week and he's just gone and ruined it. I'm pissed and it's hard to hold my speed down as they gain on me. I won't forget this and the club will be lucky if they eat a good meal for the rest of the week.

The bikes are a hundred feet behind me when my back window explodes and my shoulder catches fire. Fuck, they shot me. I can't control the car and swerve off the road heading down a small embankment into desert scrubs. I slam my foot against the brake and come to a stop. Someone's trying to kill me. The men on the bikes can't belong to Dagger.

My shoulder screams as I try to unbuckle the belt with my other hand. I need to get away. The sun shines into the vehicle and I can see very little outside.

I grab the door handle as soon as the belt is undone. Before I can open the door it's wrenched from my fingers and someone drags me out. I kick and punch with my good hand until a heavy blow hits the side of my jaw. It stuns me. The asshole has no idea who he's messing with. The second biker tries to grab my legs, but I land a nice kick to his upper thigh. Too bad I missed his cajones. If he gives me another chance, I won't.

"Fucking bitch," he yells.

The other man tosses me to the ground and cactus needles pierce my arms and back. The man I kicked boots me in the ribs and I roll, trying to protect myself.

"Fucking spic. What the hell is our club fucking doing with a piece of brown meat?"

Another kick strikes my hip and the second man lands one on my chest. I would curl into a ball but one of them lifts me. I can no longer keep track of who's who. They turn me into a human punching bag. I have no doubt they plan to kill me. I'm losing blood from the shoulder wound and the sun has a dark ring around it. A fist hits my eyes and another my nose. My breasts, stomach, and ribs take their share of hits. The pain diminishes and it's like I'm looking down from above my body watching them beat me to death.

This is how I die. I always thought it would be this way. Violence begets violence.

"*Sofia Guadalupe, you're a fighter. You fight for you and the babies.*" My mother's voice drifts through my head. I'll be with my sister and brother soon.

*Oh, Dax. I never told you I love you.*

# 30

*Dax*

**I wasn't worried when** Sofia had been gone for three hours. An hour to Globe and an hour back meant she hit the county office, dropped the papers, maybe talked to someone there for a short time, and then filled up her car before hitting the road again. It was after the fourth hour that I began to worry. Now it's after six in the evening and the county offices are closed.

I can't sit still, so I'm pacing in the front room of the clubhouse. All but a few of the brothers are here. We *were* celebrating a second chance to put our plans in motion. Now everyone's mostly quiet. No one says she took off, but I know they're thinking it.

I'm a stupid fuck.

"This is bullshit, that girl hasn't left us high and dry," Red finally grinds out. "You're all assholes for even thinking it."

I stop and turn around. "Hell. She should be here."

Red stands and faces me. "What about a car accident? Have you thought of that?"

I bring my hand over my stubby crop of hair in frustration. "It's not exactly an accident-prone trip from here to Globe."

"Okay, a blown tire, mechanical failure. Does she have her phone?"

Fuck, I didn't think about a phone. "No." I turn to Skull. "You and I are heading out. We'll check the road from here to Globe."

Skull rises and then Bear speaks up. "I'm in too. I agree with Red. She didn't leave."

I look at my brothers. "Who's in?"

They all stand.

"Let's ride," I tell them.

Five minutes later we hit the pavement with colors on full display. There are seven of us, including Rufus. It sucks that we've needed a ride and it's Sofia's absence that takes us out of the clubhouse. No matter how this turns out, we're taking a weekend ride as soon as possible.

The engines humming beside me are music. My cut flapping in the wind and the sun beating on my back feel like freedom. This is what the Crows are all about.

We hit the Globe turnoff and pick up speed. It's a lonely section of highway. Having my brothers beside me keeps me sane. I don't want Sofia to have run into car trouble. I also can't face the possibility that she left. She was too excited about filing the papers. Fuck, I need to find her.

Twenty minutes into the ride, I see flashing lights ahead of us and my muscles clench. A white truck is the only non-emergency vehicle that I can see. We roll closer and I see Sofia's car about twenty yards from the road and down a slight embankment.

I'm off my bike and running toward the car, when a deputy stops me.

"Whoa, you need to stay back," he commands.

I twist away from the hand he places on my arm. "That's my old lady's car."

He grabs me and Skull grabs my other arm.

"You need to stay back. Emergency services are working on her. They've called in a helicopter."

"What the fuck?" I shrug both hands off me.

"Look," the deputy says, "she's in bad shape. Let them do their job and talk to me."

My brain is racing. "Did she go through the windshield?" It's all I can think of. I don't see another damaged vehicle and a trip down a short hill wouldn't hurt her.

"Step over here," the deputy says in a sympathetic voice.

He isn't one of the cops from the search warrant. I know he's aware of who we are. Hell, our cuts point it out loud and clear. His tone is concerned without the usual sneer we run into. I let him lead me to his vehicle.

"Got your back, brother," Skull calls.

The deputy gives me a level look and lays out what's happening. "She's been shot and beaten within an inch of her life. The fellow in the white truck saw the car off the road and called 911. Now that you've shown up, I'm guessing this is gang related."

"It can't be. Hell," I say and place my hand on my head. It easily can be. I never talk to cops... never. I'm about to break the code. "I took over the club over a month ago. Several didn't like the new leadership and left. We have no trouble with anyone else and we're trying to clean our shit up. Fuck." I'm breathing hard and feel vomit rise in my throat. "I need to see her." I've never begged a cop for anything either.

"I need names."

"I'll give you names, just let me see her."

He takes off his hat and wipes his brow before placing it back on his head. "The car is evidence. Bullet hole in the back window and through the front seat. Don't touch anything and I'll take you down there."

"Thank you," is all I can manage to say.

He walks me past my brothers and several hit my back as I follow the deputy. They hang back as we head toward the car and the team working around a stretcher. They have an IV line in the back of her hand, and her mouth and nose are covered by an oxygen mask. Between the blood and swelling, she's unrecognizable.

"This is her boyfriend," the deputy says. "Can you let him closer?"

One of the women steps back and I'm able to drop to a knee and touch her hand. Her shirt is off with one of the crew holding a thick pad to her shoulder. Small square pads are stuck on the skin of her chest and I follow the leads to a machine that shows she's alive.

The woman who moved aside places her hand on my shoulder. "The helicopter is coming in. We need you to move back and let us take care of her. She's in good hands." She hands me Sofia's purse. "Keep this. We have her driver's license information. She's being medevaced to Phoenix General. They have a top-notch trauma team."

Sofia's face is blurry and I realize I'm crying. I wipe my eyes and bend down farther and kiss her hand. It's the only place I'm not worried about touching. "Can I go on the helicopter?" I ask.

"No, life support personnel only. I'm sorry." I can hear the chopper now. "Cover your eyes," the woman tells me. "This will move really quickly, and you need to step back," she says over the roar of the blades.

Fuck, this is Savannah all over again.

"Head to the hospital. I'll be there and wait for you to arrive," the woman assures me.

I finally take a good look at her. She's somewhere in her forties and I read compassion in her eyes, which are only partially shielded from the blowing dust. "Thank you. I'll be there as soon as possible." I stand and look one last time at the woman I love. "Her name's Sofia Guadalupe Acosta. It's a name to be proud of. She's a fighter."

The woman smiles. "A fighter is good. I'll see you at the hospital." She moves in and takes my place. I stand back as they pick up the stretcher and run for the helicopter. They move as a single unit. I watch as they load Sofia on board, and I stay where I am until the helicopter takes off.

"Do you have a notepad?" I ask the deputy. He removes one and hands it to me along with his pen. I write down one man's name and hand it back.

"Find him before I do because I'll kill him."

The deputy says nothing as I head to my bike. The brothers follow. "They're taking her to Phoenix General. She's been shot and beat. My guess is Oho. I gave his name to the deputy. Doesn't matter. I hope I find him first."

"We ride for Phoenix?" Skull asks.

"Half the men stay behind. We need to keep the other women safe. I'm taking off from here. Have someone pick up my helmet and bring it down in the truck along with some clothes. Bring Red too."

Skull takes over, which is a good thing. "Vamp, Rufus—ride with the prez." I rev my bike. Skull's hand lands on my shoulder. "She's tough. She'll be okay, Dax."

He didn't see her. I've been through this before. I turn my bike around and we take off.

# 31

*Dax*

**Sofia is in surgery** when we arrive at the hospital two hours later. The woman who helped me at the scene is Helen. She's waiting as promised.

"Sofia's in good hands. They're removing the bullet and have a plastic surgeon available for the damage to her face. Broken jaw and eye socket showed in the x-rays. This guy's good and he'll have her as pretty as she was before."

I'm barely following what she says. "You think she'll make it?"

She gives me a soft smile. "You said she's a fighter. If she is, she'll pull through."

"Did she wake up?"

"No. They don't think she has head trauma, but they won't count it out until they're sure. The doctor will come out and talk to you when surgery's over. Does she have other family?"

"No, just the club. We're her family."

"Tell the medical staff you're married and they'll give you updates and let you in the room when she's out of recovery. Don't tell anyone I told you that. I'll let the nurses know her husband is here."

I want to hug this woman. I'm not accustomed to people being nice for the sake of being nice. "Thank you," I say because there really is nothing else I can say. I won't forget what she's done.

Helen walks over to the nurses' station, talks to them for a moment, and points at me before leaving with a small wave in my direction. Vamp, Rufus, and I take over some chairs in the waiting room and kick back. An hour later, Vamp heads off to get us something to eat from a vending machine. There's a watercooler against the wall and we've stayed hydrated with the little cone cups. I walk over and check in with the nurses' station.

"I'll go check, Mr. Acosta. It will only take a minute. Wait right here."

I watch her leave and for the first time since Sofia went missing, a smile tips my lips. *Mr. Acosta*. Karma at its finest. The nurse returns a few minutes later.

"They removed the bullet first. They're working on facial reconstruction now. It's taking longer than expected because of bone grafts. She's in serious but stable condition. Surgery should wrap up in the next hour or so. She'll be in recovery for a few hours after that. As soon as she has a room, we'll get you into see her."

I breathe a sigh of relief and walk away. Vamp comes back into the waiting room with chips and candy bars. "Take these and I'll go back for liquid gold."

I relay what the nurse told me.

"We'll find him, Dagger. Don't waste time thinking about that scum. He's a dead man."

I nod and he leaves to buy coffee. Everything points to Oho. Until we know for sure, though, I won't endanger the club by sending them after him. I also want the pleasure myself. Sofia holds the answers. She holds my heart too and I need her to come back to me. The thoughts of Savannah drag me under and I'm having trouble separating the two. If Sofia dies, I'll spend the rest of my life in prison for what I do to the man who did this to her. My life will no longer matter.

Sofia pulls through surgery. The doctor looks exhausted.

"She's in serious condition. She's stabilized, but the biggest worry we have right now is the baby."

Baby?

The doctor gives me a level look. "I'm not surprised you didn't know. She's most likely only a few weeks along. It's standard to do a pregnancy test on women before we go into surgery. Her body is fighting to keep the baby. We discussed whether it was more dangerous to continue the pregnancy or let her body decide. I'm sorry. The possibility is very real that she'll miscarry. These next forty-eight hours are critical if there's any hope that she keeps the child."

I cover my eyes. Fuck, a baby. I look back at the doctor. "Her life comes first."

"Yes, it does, and if she shows signs that the baby is endangering her life, we'll do what must be done."

I nod. I can't say anything more, I'm emotionally wrung out. I keep thinking about my promise to keep her safe and never allow anyone to lay a hand on her. My fucking promise meant nothing. I told Savannah I'd take care of her too.

They give Sofia a room a few hours later. It's monitored by a central glass nurses' station built in the form of an octagon with doors leading to four separate patient rooms. Sofia will be in here until she and the baby are out of the woods. There's a single uncomfortable chair in the room, which I take over. She has so many wires and tubes that it's hard to find a place to touch her. I settle on her cold fingers. Bandages cover her head and face, including one eye. They told me the pain meds will keep her unconscious until sometime tomorrow. I don't even question what damage they could do to the baby. Sofia is all I care about. Sometime in the early morning hours I fall asleep with my head resting on the bed beside her hip. The nurses check her IV lines and vital signs every hour. They assure me in soft voices that she's holding her own.

A nurses' aide brings me breakfast at seven and I send a text to Skull. He texts back that he's out in the waiting room with Red. I scarf down the food, kiss Sofia's fingers, and head out to speak with him.

Red throws her arms around me when I walk in. I hold her tightly while she cries. Charlie is here too and she switches places with Red when Red gets herself under control.

"Thank you for coming too, Charlie," I whisper.

"That girl's family. We take care of family."

I sit and talk to them for about five minutes. They have two hotel rooms close to the hospital. I'm staying here. I don't mention the baby. It's between me and Sofia. If she loses the child, I'll leave it to her to explain if she wants to. As horrible as it sounds, I can live with it if it means Sofia survives.

I sleep off and on throughout the day. A low groan wakes me in the late afternoon. The nurse walks in. They have her vitals on a screen in the nurses' station and I can see by the screen in the room that her pulse is racing.

"It's the pain," the nurse tells me as she adds medication to one of the IVs. "It's actually a good sign and we'll taper off the meds as she starts responding. You can talk to her too. She needs to know you're here."

The nurse checks her over and leaves the room. I sit back down and hold Sofia's fingers again. "Hey, princess. Your family is here. Well, some of them stayed back at the club." Fuck, I feel like an idiot. "I'm here. I'm not leaving you." It's all I can take and my tears spill over. I lean my head against her hand and cry. I want to tell her about the baby, but I'm too afraid she'll lose it. "I love you," I whisper instead. "I never told you about Savannah. I promise I will as soon as you're back with me. She would have loved you too. She's watching over you now. She knows I can't lose another woman I love." I allow the tears to flow for both women. I never cried over Savannah or my son. My anger at the world held the tears away. They deserved my tears. Sofia deserves my tears.

It's late that night before Sofia shows more signs of life. Her moan is longer this time and I begin talking to her right away. "You're in the hospital, princess. I'm here with you, and Red and Charlie are out in the waiting room." I think they left hours ago, actually, but I want Sofia to know her family loves her enough to be here with her. Her fingers move just a bit and I give them a squeeze. "The nurse will give you more pain medicine so you'll sleep. You need to get better so we can take a ride with the club. We'll go to the river and tube down." A different nurse enters and smiles at me. I smile back while she administers more medication.

Sofia's fingers move against mine. "That's it, princess. Relax, sleep, and get well. I'm not going anywhere."

The next day is much of the same. She still has the baby. The doctor told me it's a very positive sign. I also know more about her injuries. Her jaw is wired shut and her shattered eye socket has been rebuilt. She has several broken ribs and they removed her spleen. The bullet was the least of the damage. She'll have a scar on her shoulder. The plastic surgeon came in and told me her face will heal and there will be minimal scarring. Like I care. I just want her back.

I've told her a hundred times over the last two days that I love her. I can only hope she hears me.

# 32

*Sofia*

**The pain proves I'm** alive. Dagger's voice keeps me that way. He tells me I'm in the hospital. He tells me he loves me. I can't open my eyes and I can't feel my body. It scares me. I focus on my feet and move them a few inches.

"Relax, princess." He's holding my hand. "You have bandages on your face and covering one eye. Your other is still swollen shut. I've got you. The doctors and nurses are wonderful and they've taken good care of you."

I focus some more and squeeze his fingers.

I hear another voice, a woman. "We can give you more pain medicine if you need it. Let's try one finger for yes and two for no."

Dagger releases my hand and I concentrate. Two for no. My brain finally connects to two fingers and I move them.

"I think she needs the medicine," Dagger says.

"We'll give her a little time and then give the injection. She understands what we're asking and that's the main thing. Let her judge her pain."

Dagger's rough skin wraps around my hand again. "That nurse is as stubborn as you are. I'll give it fifteen minutes and then I'm lying for you."

I can't make my brain work good enough to laugh. He tells me about my injuries explaining why I can't see or move my jaw. I appreciate it and hope I remember what he tells me. Most of all, I love the sound of his voice. The pain gets worse and when he asks me to tell him if I need meds, I lift my middle finger.

His rumble of laughter warms my heart. I drift back to sleep when the nurse leaves the room. Dagger holds my hand as my mind goes blank again.

I have no idea how much time has passed. They move me to a private room. I fight the pain meds and try to make it as long as I can. Dagger is wonderful about everything but that. I can't communicate with more than my fingers, but I can finally see out of my good eye. Dagger does a lot of pacing when he thinks I need meds.

Red and Charlie visit. They don't stay long. They tell me the clubhouse is safe and the brothers are coming to the hospital in shifts to check on me themselves. I appreciate all they tell me. I'm exhausted when they leave. Dagger comes back in. His chin scruff is a short, mangy beard now. He needs to shave. With his hair, he looks like a mental asylum reject.

I let them knock me out with pain meds because of him. He drives me crazy with his pacing.

The next day, the plastic surgeon removes my facial bandages. He has me speak, which is extremely difficult with my jaw wired. They'll remove the wires in about three weeks. It will be two weeks after that before I can use my jaw to eat. Today is the first time I've actually missed food, so it sucks and I'm crabby.

"We want you up and walking around," the doctor tells me. "A nurse will come in and remove the catheter."

Thank God. I'm tired of the nurses checking between my legs.

"We'll keep the IV in for at least another day," the doctor says. "The most important thing is that you don't fall and cause further damage to your face. If you have dizziness, sit down. Your husband can help support you today. Try a few steps on your own tomorrow."

"What about the pain meds?" Dagger asks the doctor.

I growl.

"As needed. You do need them." He gives me a pointed look. "Your body needs a chance to heal and will heal faster with minimal stress. Pain medication removes the stress. A police detective has called every day to interview you about what happened. I've put him off but no longer have a reason to."

I nod and let the doctor know I'm okay with it.

Dagger walks out with the doctor when the examination is over. I can see them talking in the hall. I can't hear, though, and it pisses me off. Dagger comes back in and sits on the side of the bed.

"What did the doctor say?" I mumble sloppily.

Dagger leans over and kisses my forehead. "That I need to talk to you about the baby." I stare into Dagger's eyes trying to piece together what he just said. "I didn't tell you before because there was a good chance you would lose the baby and I didn't want you worrying about it."

My hand moves to my stomach as realization dawns. Dagger's hand covers mine.

"You aren't far along, a few weeks only. They gave you a pregnancy test before surgery and a second one yesterday. This little tyke likes where he's at and the doctor says everything should progress normally." Tears run down my face and Dagger wipes them away. "I'll be honest. I didn't care about the baby. I was more worried about you. Doesn't mean I won't love him or her but you come first. Fuck, Sofia, I love you."

He leans in against me so my head is on his shoulder while I cry. A baby has never been part of my plans, and I don't know what the hell I'm going to do. I take a quarterly shot so I don't get pregnant. I guess I was past due for the shot and it's not like we ever used protection. Stupid, I know. Dagger releases me when my tears run their course. He takes the chair by the bed and rests his hand on my stomach.

"I need to explain about my wife, Savannah, and also about our son."

Hell, Dagger has a son. I knew he was married before, but I knew nothing about a child. I place my hand on his and squeeze his fingers.

"Savannah's parents were wealthy and they hated me. She didn't care..."

Dagger tells me everything. His son who died, Savannah, and also killing the man who took their lives. I can't help my tears. They say pregnant women cry. I'm learning it's true.

"I was a young man then, little more than a boy. I wish I could say I shouldn't have killed that man but I can't. He took everything from me. I missed her funeral service, though. My son was buried with her and I missed it. That I do regret. I never said goodbye."

Tears run down his face and I ache for his pain.

"I need to know who hurt you. I won't act irrationally. They will pay for it, though."

"Two bikers," I manage to say. "No one I know." I give him the best description I can.

"I know who they are. We'll take care of it so you and everyone else in the club is safe."

"No prison," I mumble.

He leans over and pulls me in close. "No prison, princess. I'll be around for this baby." His phone rings. He releases me and checks it. "Need to take this call. I'll be back in a few minutes."

Dagger leaves me alone with my thoughts. My hand moves back to my stomach.

Dagger's baby.

# 33

*Dax*

**Gomez was calling. I** didn't make it out of Sofia's room and into the hallway in time to take it. I decide to walk to the parking area before calling back. I haven't heard from Moon or Gomez since leaving their home. We have unfinished business and I'm hoping for an update.

It's a little after two in the afternoon and sweltering heat rises off the black asphalt. There's a bench under a tree and I head in that direction. I don't bother sitting. I've done enough of that over the past few days.

The doctor said they're discharging Sofia in the next few days if she keeps improving. I haven't dwelled on what this will cost. It's the least of my worries right now. I stand in the shade and call Gomez.

He answers immediately. "We have her and a little extra baggage. Can you talk?"

"Yes."

"Our guys picked Pauline up in Casa Grande. One of her dealers up north pointed them in the right direction after a small amount of persuasion. They found her in a trailer with two men. Strange thing is they thought my guys were there in retaliation. Apparently they messed with the wrong Latina lady."

I'm surprised my clenched hand doesn't break the phone. "You have them?"

"Yes."

"I'm at the hospital. My old lady won't be leaving for a day or two. If you hold them, there's nothing you can't ask of me."

"I don't think you were listening before. I owe you. I don't take that lightly. These guys are going nowhere. Do you want us to go ahead and take care of Pauline?"

"No. Keep her wherever you're holding them. She needs to understand what happens if she decides to return."

"What hospital are you in?" he asks.

"Phoenix General. Sofia's fucked up and lucky to be alive. So is our baby."

Gomez is silent for a moment. "They won't enjoy the time they have left. Take care of your woman and the baby."

"Thank you. Thank you for everything." Something occurs to me. "I gave the cops the name of the guy I think is responsible. I don't want it falling back on you."

"Thanks for the heads up. Won't be a problem."

The call ends. It's hard to believe it's this fucking easy. I burn to take a ride to wherever they have Oho and Candy. It pains me that they're still breathing air.

I make it one day without added blood on my hands. Sofia is improving quickly and the next day they tell us she'll go home tomorrow. I don't say anything to Sofia about Oho or Candy. I won't tell her until we're home and I'm sure we can't be overheard.

She gives the police detective nothing. He isn't happy, but looking at her it's easy to believe she remembers nothing. Even though it's a lie. She has refused to look in the mirror since the first time she went to the bathroom. I practically held her up while she examined the damage.

"Good thing I'm not a vain person," she mumbled with her wired jaw.

Any other woman would scream the place down. Sofia is like no other woman I've ever known and that includes Savannah. It felt good to tell her about my wife and baby. She needed to know.

I leave the hospital after she falls asleep with the aid of some pain killers she grumbles about taking. I know part of the reason she's reluctant to take pain meds is her mother's addiction. Sofia is so stubborn I doubt she's at risk. I admire her for holding out as long as she does.

I call Gomez and he gives me directions to the downtown warehouse where he'll meet me. It takes about twenty minutes to get there. Gomez and Rack are waiting. Rack hands me the handgun I requested. I enter the building, walk to the back, and walk into the room where I first met Gomez. Fond memories, or maybe I should say painful ones.

Oho and Candy are on their knees with their hands tied behind their backs. Pauline is tied to a chair a few feet away. She looks worse than she did the last time I saw her. I'm surprised her skin doesn't split open. I doubt she weighs eighty pounds.

I walk in front of Oho holding the gun at my hip. He knows what's coming.

"You fucking dick," he says while Candy cries. "Fuck you and fuck the woman we killed. I hope she meant something to you. Fucking brown bitch should never have been alive to leave the clubhouse. The guys will turn on you. Every fucking one of them. They won't hold with no spic."

I kick him in the stomach and he goes down. I nod at Rack and he pulls Oho back to his knees. Pauline is crying too but even she isn't as big a pussy as Candy.

"Shouldn't pick on women or children, asshole," I say before lifting the gun and putting a bullet between Candy's eyes. I didn't come here to play games. I turn the barrel of the gun to Oho. "My old lady is alive and so is my child. Two of you pussies couldn't kill her. We'll never think of you again and neither will a single member of the Crows. I'll see in you hell one day, though, and you better run and hide." I pull the trigger.

Pauline is screaming when I head to her next.

"No, Dagger, no. They never told me. I fucking didn't know," she pleads.

I lift the gun and rest the barrel against her forehead. "If I ever see you again, I'll kill you. If you ever step foot in the state of Arizona, I'll know. Do you get me, Pauline?"

"Yes, I swear. I swear."

I hand the gun to Gomez on my way out. We don't say a word. Justice has been served.

I sleep the last night at the hospital with Sofia. It will be wonderful to go home tomorrow. Red assured me the women have done a damn good job of cleaning my bedroom and bathroom so Sofia is comfortable.

I go to admitting to fill out the papers for the hospital bill. They hand me the paperwork and I scan the itemized total as it stands. It's over six hundred thousand dollars.

"Sign at the bottom and you're good to go," the woman tells me.

I shake my head. "I can't make more than a small down payment on this right now."

"Well, um… the bill's been paid in full. We have a PO box listed here to send follow up bills to for payment."

"What?"

She hands me the paper stating the bill is paid in full. "Whoever paid didn't sign and we need your signature for discharge."

I look at the address. It's in Phoenix and I know it was Gomez or Moon who paid this. Fuck. How do I ever say thank you?

I sign the papers and head back up to Sofia's room to get her the hell out of this place.

# 34

*Sofia*

**I'm a horrible patient**. Dagger bought a car with really good air conditioning to replace mine and he's driving me to another medical appointment. The oral surgeon is removing the wires from my jaw today. I'm so relieved. They've had me on anti-nausea medication because of the pregnancy and the possibility of throwing up. It makes me drowsy and I hate it. I'm also tired of eating from a straw.

My man's cock hasn't been down my throat since the accident. This does not improve my mood. Dagger refuses to touch me in any way until the doctor gives the all clear. Yeah, that doesn't improve my mood either. If the oral surgeon can't give the go-ahead, Dagger will be driving me back to the hospital so I can find the surgeon who removed the bullet. Someone will give the all clear for sex today or someone will die.

I'm also tired of everyone treating me like the princess they call me. Fuck that shit. I'm going to punch someone. Having the wires removed is no fun and my jaw aches like a motherfucker when we leave.

Dagger keeps looking at me and grinning.

"What?" I finally ask.

"I can't believe you asked him when it was safe to put my dick in your mouth. Poor guy almost had a stroke." Dagger starts laughing and it's over a minute before he quiets down.

"Doctors should know not to get between a Latina woman and her man. He said we could have sex too." My speech is somewhat better, but I'm almost afraid to open my jaw too far.

"Yeah, after he called an obstetrician."

"If you don't want sex, just say so. I'm sure I can find someone else to scratch my itch."

"Fuck that. You're mine, princess." He takes my hand and moves it to the front of his jeans. "Don't ever think I don't want you."

His cock is hard and I squeeze. He groans and I smile.

Rufus picked up the mail while we were at the medical appointment, and the papers from the county are waiting for us when we arrive back at the clubhouse.

Dagger pulls me into his lap and circles his arms around me. The envelope is in front of us. "Open it," he whispers in my ear.

"Damn. What if it's bad news?"

"Then we sic your Latina ass on them and they'll be sorry. Open it."

My fingers actually tremble as I tear open the envelope. We begin reading.

"You did it, princess."

"Hell. It's approved."

Dagger stands up, puts me on my feet, and lets out a loud yell. "Fuck yeah, we're in business." He's careful of my ribs as he pulls me in close. I can't keep a stupid grin from my face. "Call the brothers, Rufus. We're partying tonight."

His forehead leans against mine. "I love you," he whispers. "Didn't matter what the papers said." His hand wiggles between us and goes into his pocket. When he pulls his hand out, a gold band rests in his palm. "You can choose something else if you want. I had Savannah's ring melted down along with mine and then had two remade."

I stare at the band. I get why he did this. Savannah was his world and because of that her and their child are part of my world too. The ring represents love and he's giving it to me.  "Where's yours?" I ask in a gruff voice that has nothing to do with having the wires removed from my jaw. He reaches into his other pocket and pulls out a larger band.

I take them both with trembling fingers. Tears stream down my cheeks. I lift them to my lips and kiss them. Dagger pulls me back against him and lets me cry.

"Is that a yes?"

I'm only capable of nodding with my head buried in his chest.

"She said yes," Vampire shouts.

I forgot a few of the guys were here.

"Double party," AJ whoops.

"I love you, princess," Dagger says loud enough for everyone to hear.

I feel loved. I have a family and a baby on the way. I never knew exactly what I was searching for but now I do and I have it in spades.

We party until two in the morning. I, of course, don't drink. Taking all the drugs in the hospital bothers me and I worry for our child. I don't care what the doctors say. I don't plan to take so much as an aspirin for the rest of my pregnancy.

I'm exhausted and trying to keep my eyes open when Dagger lifts me and carries me to our room. He lays me down, removes my shoes, and quickly takes my clothes off.

"Mmm," I say with sleepy eyes while he massages my insteps. It feels so good that my back arches.

He stands and pulls the sheet over me. "Get some sleep, princess."

I'm suddenly wide awake. "No. You aren't leaving me." I throw the cover off, spread my legs, and rub my fingers along my pussy lips. "If you won't take care of my problem, I will."

His baby blues darken and I watch while he divests himself of his clothing. His eyes burn into mine and finally I know I've broken through the celibacy rule he's had in place for the past few weeks.

"You better make it good, white boy. My fingers feel pretty damn incredible."

He leans over and grabs my hand, lifting my wet fingers to his lips. "You taste damn incredible too."

"Fuck me, Dax, fuck me until I scream your name."

"I don't want to hurt you, princess." I'm about to protest, when he continues. "You tell me if something feels uncomfortable, deal?"

"Yes," I say quietly.

He moves over me. His arms hold him up as he rolls to my other side and brings me on top of him. "Ride me, baby," he groans as I rub myself along his cock.

He's hard, which is never a surprise. My face still has yellow bruises. The stitches came out a few days ago, but my face is still puffy around the bone implant. He looks at me like I'm beautiful. His kind of beautiful. I lift to my knees and position myself so I can sink down on his cock. I place my hands on his chest and slowly lift my hips, lower them, and lift. Our eyes remain locked. So much love.

God, I've missed this. There's no connection on earth that even comes close.

"You're beautiful, princess."

I smile widely. My jaw aches, but I don't care. My goal is to suck his cock in a week. My smile goes wider and he lifts his hands to my breasts. I move my hands back to his thighs and increase my speed, loving his heavy breathing and knowing I drive him as crazy as he drives me.

I'm there much too quickly and pulse around his cock.

"Dax," I cry.

"Gotcha, princess."

"Dax come with me. God, please."

"I'm there," he pants.

And he is. His warmth fills me. His touch sears. My body burns.

I wake up with the most incredible sensation between my legs. Dagger has my knees over his shoulders while he eats my pussy. I slept through his arranging me, but God there's no way I could sleep through this.

He locks eyes with mine and smiles after releasing my clit from between his lips. "You taste so fucking good, princess. Sweeter. It's the baby, gotta be."

"It's you. You're sweeter," I tell him and groan when he slides his tongue inside me.

I love him so much. Love his nasty sexual appetite and how much it turns me on. I need to ask the doctor about pregnancy and anal, I think, before I can't think at all.

# 35

*Dax*

**Today is Sofia's first** ultrasound and I can't help remembering the last day I had with Savannah. This is bittersweet and Sofia understands.

Dr. Andreas walks in the room and takes a seat by Sofia. She's an older Latina doctor in her sixties and Sofia loves her. She wanted a doctor who would be accepting of our lifestyle. I wasn't happy when the doctor said Sofia could ride on the back of my bike with a helmet for as long as she was comfortable. No, not happy at all.

The club took a ride last weekend to Flagstaff and I was a wreck the entire time. Sofia laughed when I cussed out a driver for moving too close to our ass before passing. It was an old woman, and someone needed to report her so she has her eyes re-examined.

The doctor places clear jell on the ultrasound wand before placing it on Sofia's belly.

Sofia laughs and says, "It's cold."

I smile, lean down, and kiss her cheek. "Buck up, princess."

We watch the picture on the screen as the doctor moves the wand around to locate the baby.

"I expected this. Your hCG levels were high, so I'm not at all surprised."

Sofia tries to sit up. "What?" she asks in rising panic.

"No worries. Stay still and I'll show you." The doctor moves the wand again.

Sofia sinks back against the bed, but her body stays tense. I'm holding her hand and her fingernails dig into my skin.

"See here," the doctor says, "here's the heartbeat." She moves the wand again. "And here's the other heartbeat. You're having twins."

"Fuck," I whisper.

"Yes, Mr. Montgomery, that's what usually gets you into this situation."

Our doctor has a sense of humor. I take my eyes from the monitor and turn to Sofia. She's crying. "My mother told me there were two. I thought she was talking about my sister and brother."

My wife has gone a little loco, but she's pregnant with twins, so I guess I better get used to it.

"The babies are healthy. Good heartbeats and good size. We'll be monitoring you closely and I'm afraid I have a different opinion about the motorcycle rides now. Twins can come into this world without any complications, but we need to help that along."

"I love you, Dr. Andreas," I tell her.

"Of course you do," my wife says. "She's giving you your way."

The doctor laughs and Sofia grumbles.

"Do you want a picture?" the doctor asks. "It will be at least another month before we can distinguish the sex of the babies."

"Please," Sofia says quietly.

We leave the doctor's office with two pictures. Because we were coming to the city, I insisted on bringing the car. Before I open her door, I pull her into my arms. "I don't know if I can handle twins." I thread my fingers into her hair and kiss her.

"You will be a wonderful father." She puts her lips against mine again and then leans away. "I need a favor."

"Anything, princess."

We find the building that suits her needs and I follow her inside. The interior is shadowed. I feel uncomfortable, but Sofia keeps a tight hold on my hands and pulls me forward with her. We're in a small Catholic church so my wife can light candles for her mother, siblings, Savannah, and our babies.

She explained in the car about her mother talking to her before she lost consciousness. I have no doubt Sofia believes she did. I won't argue. I sink to my knees beside her when she tugs my hand. She closes her eyes and prays.

A Justice of the Peace in Phoenix married us two weeks ago. I never thought about a church wedding. Sofia never said anything about it either. The harmony of the church settles over me and I understand the draw Sofia feels. I swear I smell the faint scent of Savannah's perfume when I close my eyes and add my own prayer for Sofia and the babies.

We stay for about twenty minutes. Sofia lights her candles and I leave a donation. I'm glad we came.

*Seven months later...*

Our son and daughter were born at full term. They're healthy and perfect. I walk out to the waiting room. Every member of the club and their women are here. Sofia was in labor for almost twenty-four hours and it's been an incredibly long night.

I can't stop the grin that splits my face when Skull stands up and walks over to me. "Boy and girl. Both healthy and Sofia is exhausted but doing well."

He throws his arms around me and pounds his ham hocks into my back. "Fuck, Dagger. Congratulations."

Cheers go up.

"I need to get back. Love you, brother," I say with my own slap on his back.

The Desert Crows just increased by two.

I walk back into Sofia's room. The babies are resting in her arms and I slip my hands beneath our daughter and bring her to my chest. I know who I'm holding by the color of her head cap. This is Masey Savannah Montgomery. Sofia is holding our son, Jonathan Dax Montgomery. We've visited Savanah's and Mason's grave several times in the past few months. I'll make a special trip and tell Mason all about his new sister and brother. I need him and Savannah watching over them.

Sofia's smile is beautiful but tired.

"I'll hold them both while you sleep. You did a good job, momma," I whisper.

"I'm sorry I cussed at you," she says with another sleepy smile.

"Like every other day," I tease.

Her brown eyes stare into mine. "I love you, Dax."

I hold the baby closer and lean over to kiss her sweet lips. "Thank you, princess. I love you too."

### Sofia

Strange that it's motherhood that changes me the most. Do I still have anger issues? Yes. Am I learning to control myself? Yes. Dax, Masey and Jonathan are my lifeline and the Crows put me in my place when needed. The men and women of the club take my shit with a smile that has me feeling foolish. They've learned to kill me with kindness. It works. I pull the rage in and try to leave the room before smiling back. Bottom line—this is what family is all about.

I love my children in a way that's impossible to describe. I see this fierce love in Dax's eyes when he looks at the three of us. We live in a dangerous world and it will take us both to keep our children safe. Dax has done so much to lead the Crows out of illegal activity. He's also pulled the club into legal medical marijuana and teamed with Moon's organization to do it. This *conversation* took place before the babies were born. I about screamed the clubhouse down because I resisted the idea. Now Red and I have two dispensaries in our names. Dax couldn't move forward without our clean criminal histories. He spent an entire morning with his face between my thighs to convince me this was the right move for us.

What can I say? The man has a way without words.

### Dax

The babies are growing like weeds and our lives weren't complete without them. The store and repair shop opened a few months ago. We have more business than we can handle. The clubhouse is undergoing major repairs right now. Sofia is getting a brand-new kitchen that's essential for all the mouths she feeds. Tramp hooked up with one of the brothers and she's an old lady now. She's also Sofia's chief assistant when it comes to meals. All the ladies take turns with the babies with Red watching closely. She insists that Masey and Jonathan will call her grandma.

My son and daughter have their mother's dark eyes and hair. They're perfect.

This morning is the first time Sofia is willing to leave the babies and join the club for a ride. Curly Sue and Red stay behind to watch the kids. Everyone else is with us. Sofia has her own cut now declaring she's a Desert Crow. I'm so proud to have her arms wrapped tightly around my waist.

She's changed and though she worried about becoming a mother, she's incredible. I never had a doubt. Sofia is the mother of the entire club. She fills these shoes with an iron fist, vocal cords that bring the roof down, and more love then most of the club has ever experienced.

Before Savannah died, I was having artwork tattooed on my back to show my love for my wife and son. It remained unfinished and I had the tat put on my chest to honor my wife and son when I got out of prison. After Sofia married me, I had the club's emblem tattooed over the work on my back. Sofia, my babies, and the Crows are my family.

It's a beautiful morning. The wind is at our backs and sun on our faces.

Desert Crows forever, forever Desert Crows.

Dear reader,

Before anyone yells at me for knocking foster parents, I want you to know I have worked with incredible foster parents and also ones on the other end of the spectrum. For the purposes of this story, Sofia's interactions were not the best. If you are a foster parent please know I admire you greatly!

I knew when I typed "The End" that not everyone would love Sofia as much as me. She's hard to love. Her character is based on a case I had as a detective with a young Latina woman. I can't go into a lot of detail but I gave her a break due to her childhood history and yes, she spent a lot of time in the foster care system. A few years later, she came into the police department and asked me for a reference to become a nurse. I gave her the reference and she's never looked back. She treated my mother in the emergency room once and I couldn't believe her compassion. Hers is not Sofia's story but the anger of our first interaction was quite similar. Sofia fought with me throughout the book and I had to rewriter her three times to get it right. Several characters in this book represent a woman who pulled herself out of hell and made a life for herself and her children. I hope I did her justice.

What can I say? Dax is part fantasy and I'll leave it at that.

Using the "N" word was extremely difficult for me. I backed myself into a corner writing about a skinhead motorcycle club and I couldn't see how to keep it real and not cross my own personal line. Thank you Sherma for reading the scene and offering reassurance.

Thank you to Bobbi for walking me through Meth addiction withdrawals. You are always an inspiration.

For anyone skeptical that prison inmate/white supremacists can't change, you're wrong. I saw it with my own eyes and it gives me hope. ANYONE can change!

Fact check 1: Bestiality is profiled as a white crime and so are serial killers. I worked both cases as a detective. Yep, white.

Fact check 2: The Lady of Guadeloupe Mission Sofia stops at in New Mexico is actually the description of the San Rafael Catholic Mission in Concho, Arizona. It's a beautiful small historical landmark and worth stopping to see.

Fact check 3: All Bikes in Rye, Arizona with over 9000 bikes burned in 2013.

Fact check 4: Arizona Red Bottom Chili is my husband's specialty and I had to add it to the book. It's damn HOT!

Fact check 5: The Tzeltal Maya people were removed from their homes in the rainforest in 1971 by the Mexican government. It's an incredibly sad history of an amazing culture.

Peace, love & hope,
Holly

Find me on social media. The best way to keep track of my world is by joining the Wicked Book Newsletter. A FREE copy of Crimson Warrior is included.

Newsletter: http://eepurl.com/bQ66U5
Facebook: http://facebook.com/hollysrobertsauthor
Twitter: http://twitter.com/mywickedstories
Instagram: http://instagram.com/wicked_story_telling
Website: http://wickedstorytelling.com
Email: wickedstorytelling@gmail.com

# Bibliography

Writing as Holly S. Roberts

Hotter Than Hell Series – Outlaw Romance
Heat
Sizzle
Burn
Ignite

Completion Series – New Adult Romance
Play (free ebook)
Strike
Kick
Slam
Ruck
Stick

Crimson Series – Vampire Erotic Romance
Crimson Warrior
Crimson Brothers

Club El Diablo Series – Kinky Romance
One Dom at a Time (free ebook)
Piercing a Doms Heart
Touched by a Dom
Domination in Pink
Two Doms for Angel (Angel's Doms)
Caught by Two Doms (Angel's Doms)
Bad Boy Dom (Bad Boys of Rock)
Loving Two Doms (Bad Boys of Rock)
Temporary Dom (Bad Boys of Rock)

Writing as D'Elen McClain

Fang Chronicles – Paranormal Romance
Amy's Story (free ebook)

Emily's Story
Zenya's Story
Mandy's Story
Dmitri
Ivan
Tyboll
Esha's Story

Fire Chronicles – Paranormal Romance
Dragons Don't Cry (free ebook)
Dragons Don't Love
Dragons Don't Forgive
Dragons Live Forever
Dragons Don't Give a Damn (coming soon)

Writing as Suzie Ivy

Bad Luck Detective Series – Police Humor/Inspirational/Memoir
Bad Luck Cadet & Officer
The Forever Team (appropriate for young adults)
Ten (a mystery thriller, coming soon)

Made in the USA
San Bernardino, CA
02 July 2016